KT-438-967

CIRCUS OF THIEVES AND THE COMEBACK CAPER

WILLIAM SUTCLIFFE
ILLUSTRATED BY DAVID TAZZYMAN

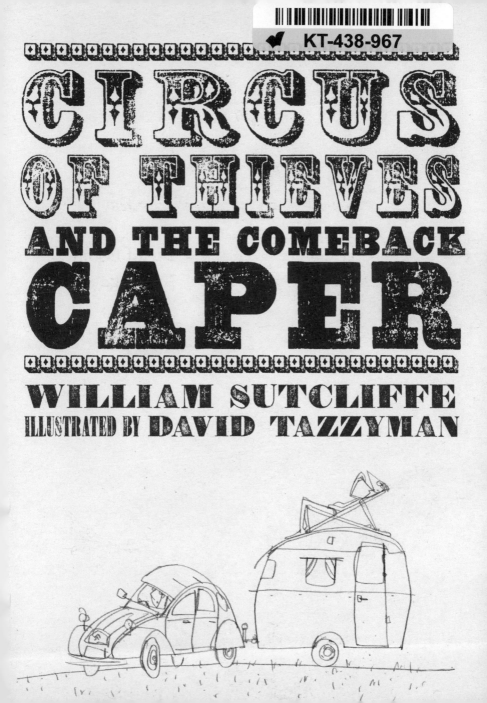

First published in Great Britain in 2016 by Simon and Schuster UK Ltd
A CBS COMPANY

Text copyright © 2016 William Sutcliffe
Illustrations copyright © 2016 David Tazzyman

This book is copyright under the Berne Convention.
No reproduction without permission.
All rights reserved.

The right of William Sutcliffe and David Tazzyman to be identified as the author
and illustrator of this work has been asserted by them in accordance with sections
77 and 78 of the Copyright, Designs and Patents Act, 1988.

1 3 5 7 9 10 8 6 4 2

Simon & Schuster UK Ltd
1st Floor, 222 Gray's Inn Road
London
WC1X 8HB

Simon & Schuster Australia, Sydney
Simon & Schuster India, New Delhi

A CIP catalogue record for this book is available from the British Library.

PB ISBN 978-1-4711-4535-3
eBook ISBN 978-1-4711-4536-0

This book is a work of fiction. Names, characters, places and incidents are either
the product of the author's imagination or are used fictitiously. Any resemblance
to actual people living or dead, events or locales is entirely coincidental.

Printed and bound by CPI Group (UK) Ltd, Croydon, CR0 4YY

Simon & Schuster UK Ltd are committed to sourcing paper that is made from wood
grown in sustainable forests and supports the Forest Stewardship Council, the
leading international forest certification organisation. Our books displaying the
FSC logo are printed on FSC certified paper.

www.simonandschuster.co.uk
www.simonandschuster.com.au

For my three caperers:
Saul, Iris and Juno – WS

For two feisty little bookworms,
Laura & Mia xx – DT

The mystery of the appearing spoon

CHILLY ISN'T IT?

I know, I know, I shouldn't grumble about the weather, but that wind just cuts right through you, doesn't it? And the rain! All that water, just falling out of the sky for absolutely no reason. What a waste!

And the mud! Just look at it.

Wait! What's that?!

If that was ordinary mud, it wouldn't be moving. It wouldn't be jiggling and wobbling, and it wouldn't . . . it certainly wouldn't . . . What on earth . . .? It's a hand! A gloopy and muddy hand, just coming up out of the ground holding a . . . could that be . . . a spoon?

Is this evolution starting all over again from the beginning? Is life emerging afresh from the primordial ooze, beginning with four fingers, a thumb and a piece of cutlery?

No – hang on a second – there's some writing on the back of the spoon, in very small letters. I can hardly read it. It seems to say, ʹPROPERTY OF HM PRISON GRIMWOOD SCRUBSʹ.

It's a prison break! In broad daylight, right in front of our very eyes, a criminal spoon is escaping!

Wait! There's something else . . . A hand and a wrist is attached to the spoon. Now a whole arm. It's an accomplice!

I think you can guess what's coming next – unless you have an unusually poor understanding of anatomy, in which case I'll give you a clue. It's not a foot.

Correct! It's a shoulder, then a head. A head so muddy that at first it looks more like an old football. But this isn't a football, since a football would be very unlikely to open a muddy mouth and shout **'F R E E E E E D O O O O O O O O O M ! WOOHOOOO! WE DONE IT!'**

The evidence is pretty conclusive, now. This escapee is neither spoon nor football, but human. With a wriggle and a squelch, a squerch and a squizzle, this human hauls himself up out of the ground, wipes the mud from his eyes, and takes a deep, happy breath. Then, displaying the disloyalty and ingratitude that is not uncommon among criminals, he tosses his trusty accomplice, the unfortunate hard-working spoon, into a bush.

Behind him, another dripping form emerges from the muck. Then another.

The three men grab at one another, jumping up and down as they engage in a slimy hug which makes the following noise: *SSHHHLLLLUP-SHHHHLGGG-SHLLLUUUUP-SHHHHLGGGG.*

'WE DONE IT!' escapee number one says again.

'WE DONE IT!' says escapee number two.

'WE DID IT!' says escapee number three. The jumping stops, and the other two stare at him, unimpressed by the way he has corrected their grammar. There is a time for grammatical pickiness, and the middle of a shlurpy filth-encrusted embrace following a daring and successful jailbreak is not it.

'Oi! If you're so posh, how come you's standing here wearing prison uniform, hugging a couple of scumbags like us?' snaps escapee number one.

'This is no time to argue,' says escapee number three, politely pretending that he hasn't heard the word "you's". 'We have to run for it. We have to find Shank.'

So they do. They run for it.

And, yes, you really did hear the dread word: Shank.

But this Shank to which they refer is not the Armitage Shank you know and loathe. Oh, no. This is another Shank entirely. Zachary Shank.

You won't have heard of Zachary Shank, unless you are a mind reader, or come from the future, or are part of the Shank clan, in which case you are fictional yourself, but if you're reading this book and you are a fictional character from the very same book, then that means . . . oh, no, my head just exploded from an overdose of weirdness.

Where was I? Zachary Shank. Of the Shank clan. With a brother whose name might ring a bell for aficionados of circus thievery.

Yes, Zachary Shank is the brother of Armitage. And not just an ordinary brother, but a twin. And not just an ordinary twin, but an identical twin. And not just an ordinary identical twin but an identical twin of surprisingly identical horribleness to the one you already know.

Believe it! There are two of them.

Revolting, I know, but I'm afraid the world can't always be kittens and rainbows and daisies and frolics in summer sunshine. Sometimes it's soggy picnics sitting on cowpats in cold drizzle, wearing shoes that leak and embarrassing trousers you've tried six times to hide in the bin. Because you probably don't need me to tell you that it can't be long before this Zachary Shank character turns up to besmirch these pages with the kind of hideous behaviour that makes decent people cover their ears and go 'LA LA LA! SORRY, I CAN'T HEAR A SINGLE WORD YOU'RE SAYING.'

This will be the Shankiest book ever written, and for those repulsive Shanks you need a strong stomach, a sturdy liver and a good chunky pair of kidneys. Read on at your peril. Prepare to be Shanked.

Our three grimy escapees ran off through the park, caking themselves in as much mud as they could in order to disguise the fact that under the mud they were wearing stripy uniforms bearing the slogan:

PROPERTY OF HM PRISON GRIMWOOD SCRUBS.

IF YOU SEE ME RUNNING AROUND WEARING THIS, CALL THE POLICE BECAUSE I AM CLEARLY A MENACE TO SOCIETY.

They had already forgotten about their trusty accomplice.

'WHAT ABOUT ME, YOU HORRIBLE, SELFISH SLUG-BUCKETS?!' yelled the spoon from under a bush. 'I THOUGHT I WAS PART OF THE CREW! YOU CAN'T LEAVE ME HERE!'

But they didn't hear him, because they didn't speak Spoon, and because spoons talk at a frequency so high it is inaudible to the human ear.

'I'LL RAT ON YOU!' shouted the angry cutlery. 'I WILL! IF A POLICE SPOON COMES PAST, I'LL TELL HIM EVERYTHING AND YOU'LL BE DONE FOR!'

The three men ran on without a backward glance, slipping away into the maze of city streets, on the trail of that East End legend, the criminal mastermind and massively devious slimeball, Zachary Shank.

Spoons are so squeaky, even forks can't hear them.

The return of Ernesto Espadrille

EVERY CLOUD HAS A SILVER LINING, They say.

They are wrong, of course. Clouds don't have linings at all. They are just cloud, right to the edge. Don't these people ever look up? Honestly, what a load of old tosh.

But the sentiment is sometimes useful. If we leave aside our irritation at the wild meteorological inaccuracy, we can perhaps entertain the idea of

Zachary Shank as a dark, looming cloud of nastiness, made a little less dark, looming and nasty by the arrival, here in Chapter Two, of the exceptionally pleasant Ernesto Espadrille.

Ah, that's better. And I have some good news for you. After two years of being unjustly imprisoned, locked away from all contact with his son Billy, and after the near-disaster of yet another false arrest during a robbery at the Oh, Wow! centre just a few months earlier, Ernesto was at last free to practise his trade again. That trade, of course, being the art of circusry.

After so long away from the circus circuit it takes a while to get going again, but Ernesto was so popular, so highly respected, so loved by everyone who had ever worked with him, that things had moved much faster than he was expecting. Already, he was only days away from the biggest night of his professional life: the relaunch of Ernesto Espadrille as a ringmaster and circus entrepreneur in his own right. Yes, it was Comeback Time.

In just forty-eight hours, Ernesto Espadrille's Extreme Extravaganza would make its debut. The star performer, apart from Ernesto himself, was his twelve-year-old son, Billy Espadrille, who until recently had been performing under the name Billy Shank.

And why would a peachy and fresh Espadrille want to go on stage in the guise of a rancid old Shank? Well, it would take me roughly two whole books to explain that properly, but the short version is this: he had no choice. Long ago, after Billy's mother died in a tragic trapeze accident, Ernesto had slowly lost his mind, then his circus. Eventually he'd simply drifted away, leaving that infamous predator Armitage Shank to 'adopt' not just Billy Espadrille, but the entire Espadrille circus. Billy had nowhere else to go, no alternative but to become a Shank. At least, he thought he had no alternative, until he met a spirited young girl by the name of Hannah. But we're getting ahead of ourselves. Or, in fact, behind ourselves. Sometimes explaining the past is like trying to untangle a plate of spaghetti. Let's just move on.

After weeks of intense rehearsal with his real father, Billy's act had lifted to a whole new level. He still conducted most of his performance while trotting around the ring on the back of Narcissus the camel, and he still performed juggling, archery and sundry acrobatics, but now there was also a magical theme. His pièce de résistance was a magic trick that hadn't been attempted by any magician anywhere. Never in the history of stage illusion had anyone ever successfully sawn a camel in half. Billy was the first, ably assisted by Narcissus (who thought the whole thing was kind of stupid, but

---

🐌 An average portion of spaghetti, fully untangled, is 37 metres long.

co-operated in return for an extra bucket of taramasalata).

As part of his comeback circus, Ernesto had recruited many of his favourite acts from when he'd been at the peak of his fame. All of them remembered him, and answered the call to rejoin the Espadrille troupe. His first recruits were the Franco-Dutch contortionist double act, Delia de la Doolah and Vonda van der Venda, who could fit themselves through a de-stringed badminton racket while knitting a woolly hat in the shape of a toaster, holding one needle each. This was an act that had to be seen to be believed, and then it was still pretty hard to credit, even if you were the lucky audience member chosen to hold the badminton racket or take away the toaster-hat. Ernesto was planning to use his contortionists as the grand opening.

They would be followed by the great Canadian

🐪 He didn't *really* cut Narcissus in half. But it did look that way. Which is, officially, an international dromedary-showbiz first.

knife-thrower, Chancey Bris, who could land a knife between the legs of his assistant, blindfolded, from ten metres. He tended to need a new assistant every week or two, since nervous breakdowns were a problem, but Bris himself had nerves of steel.

A quick turn from the prestidigitator, Bellagio Spigot, would follow that, after which came Ernesto's prize recruits, the clowns Hank and Frank, who he had pinched from Armitage Shank. They didn't take much persuading, either. In fact, the call went something like this:

ERNESTO: This is Ernesto Espadrille here. I'm starting my own circus. Would you like to join?

HANK: Oh, yes! We'd love to!

FRANK: Says who?

HANK: Me.

FRANK: What about me?

This is a magician who does clever tricks with his hands. The word comes from the latin 'digit', which means finger, and 'presti', which means, 'blooming 'eck, did you see that?'

HANK: Of course you want to. You whinge all the time about wanting a different boss.

FRANK: That doesn't mean you can answer for me.

HANK: But you want the job.

FRANK: Of course I do.

HANK: So why are you arguing?

FRANK: Why are you arguing?

HANK: Why are you arguing?

FRANK: I'm not arguing.

HANK: Yes, you are.

FRANK: No, I'm not.

HANK: Yes, you are!

FRANK: No, I'm not! ✤

ERNESTO: Ehurghehuchhuch! Guys! Do you want the job?

HANK AND FRANK: Of course we do!

ERNESTO: Er . . . great. When can you start?

FRANK: This week.

✤ This is a cough. There is much dispute in literary circles about how to spell out a cough. This dispute is of no interest, so I shan't go into details. If you really want to know more, you can read *From Hrmph to Tsk: A Guide to Noises You Can Make But Can't Spell* by **Xtrpt Pffffp**.

HANK: Next week.
FRANK: This week!
HANK: Next week!

I think we can leave the conversation there. Negotiations took a while, not so much between Ernesto and the clowns as between Hank and Frank, but they got there in the end, and the siblings were installed as the closing act of the first half.

The second half was to kick off with another recruit from Armitage's cast. Jesse was just as easy to enlist, simply by promising him that he wouldn't have to do any more human cannonballing, and that he wouldn't have to wear his polyester leopard-skin leotard any more. For Ernesto, Jesse would simply be the strongman. This wasn't hard for Jesse, since he was a strong man. His new act mainly featured Jesse ripping a car to bits with his bare hands, wearing an extremely small pair of swimming trunks with the word 'JESSE' written on the bottom. Ernesto was of the opinion that the audience wanted to see a strongman's muscles, and Jesse didn't mind as long as he got to throw away his itchy leopard-skin monstrosity. In fact, he burned it, which took about two seconds, since cheapo polyester leopard-skin is really quite astonishingly flammable. This made Jesse worry that his career as a human cannonball was even more dangerous than he had feared. A flaming human cannonball would have been spectacular but, health-wise, it was pretty much a one-off stunt.

After Jesse came the Nigerian fire-breather, Halle Tosis (who was rumoured to be a princess), then Mitzi Schnitzel and her performing puppies, who staged a canine dance routine on a tightrope wearing doggie sailor suits, culminating in a barked karaoke rendition of 'I Dreamed a Dream'. This act wasn't to everyone's taste, but Mitzi was an old friend and she needed the work.

For a change of pace, this was to be followed by the Finnish motorbike daredevil Empti Caapaak and his wife Mülti-Störi. Their three children, Shortstaï, Longstaï and Payandisplaï, had a daring role in the finale, which was a human slalom around the sides of a metal cage that filled the whole ring.

In their prime, Empti and Mülti-Störi had been indoor motocross champions, which is a sport where you ride round and round in circles very fast in front of an audience, but for some reason they found this ultimately unsatisfying, and it was only when they developed a circus routine that they became truly happy. The circus routine also consisted of riding round in circles very fast in front of an audience but, being non-competitive, it was more to their taste. The Caapaaks were old hippies at heart.

Shortstaï and Longstaï were in training to take over the act when they were older, but Payandisplaï wanted to be a marine biologist.

The show would climax in the Espadrille father-and-son double act, which was a unique combination of trapeze artistry, juggling, archery and camel-sawing.

Nobody would leave Ernesto Espadrille's Extreme Extravaganza feeling that they hadn't got their money's worth, that was for sure. If

Ernesto had a motto, it would have been 'Something For Everyone'.[⊖]

In the circus world, the return of Ernesto Espadrille was big news. Big news in a Big Top in a big park in the East End of a big city – not far, in fact, from HM Prison Grimwood Scrubs. Not far at all from a bush concealing a certain lonely and vengeful spoon.

⊖ But he didn't have a motto. He thought mottoes were stupid and pointless. If you'd twisted his arm and forced him to choose one, he probably would have chosen the phrase, 'I Hate Mottos' as his motto. Billy had once suggested that he should have badges made bearing this motto, but Ernesto wasn't interested in diversifying into the novelty accessories trade. Not even when Billy suggested printing badges that said 'I Never Wear Badges,' an idea that would have made Ernesto far richer than putting on circuses for a living.

THREE

Armitage has a mood swing

EVERY SILVER LINING HAS A CLOUD, as the old saying doesn't go. Yes, you guessed it, we're getting Shanky again. But you're going to have to wait to find out more about the grisly old grot-bucket Zachary, because now it's time to wheel out that living monument to despicability and yukitude, Armitage Shank.

The good news is that Armitage had fallen on the hard times he so amply deserved. He'd lost several of his big acts to Ernesto and generally

Shank's Impossible Circus was in a dire state. The bad news is that at some point in the next few paragraphs he will cook up a plan to revive his fortunes.

We find him sitting in his caravan, sulking, thumbing through the latest issue of *Pointless Expensive Gadgets You Must Buy*. This was his favourite magazine. It made him drool. It also made him weep, since he couldn't afford any of the

pictured gadgets. Incidentally, he also had a nasty cold, so his nose was running. This drizzle of tears, snot and drool had left the magazine in a damp and unsavoury condition.📖

Armitage was gazing through moist, envious eyeballs at a pair of underwater binoculars with built-in MP3 player, which he was now convinced he could barely live without, when his body jolted upright. In the corner of the page, he had spotted an advertisement:

ROLL UP, ROLL UP!
A CIRCUS LEGEND RETURNS TO THE STAGE! ERNESTO ESPADRILLE'S EXTREME EXTRAVAGANZA. FOR ONE NIGHT ONLY! 1ST JANUARY! HOCKNEY MARSHES! PREPARE TO BE
AMAAAAAAAAZED!!!

📖Armitage often wondered why Irrrrena would never lend him her copies of *Rich People With Good Teeth Sitting on Sofas*. **This was why.**

Armitage leaped to his feet, banging his head on the ceiling. You have to be careful in caravans. Leaping is not advised. Unless you are very short. Or are standing under an open skylight. Or are wearing a helmet. Or have applied foam padding to the ceiling.

If you've done all these things, you can go ahead and install a trampoline.

Armitage sat down again, rubbing his head with one hand and twirling his moustache with the other. Moustache-twirling was a sure sign that Armitage was a-plotting.

Ernesto Espadrille! His circus nemesis! The man who had stolen the love of his life! The man who was a superlative ringmaster and effortlessly popular and objectionably handsome and generally brilliant at everything except toenail-clipping chess! The man who'd had the audacity to steal Billy off him just because he happened to be his real father!

Armitage hated many things, but there was nothing and nobody he loathed more than Ernesto Espadrille.

Circus legend, eh? Returns to the stage, indeed?

Well, well, well. Not so fast, Mr Espadrille. Because Armitage Shank was making other plans.

Prepare to be amazed, huh?

Oh, yes. Amazed and bamboozled and swindled and stunned.

Once and for all.

This time, Ernesto would get what he deserved.

You might think Armitage had already taken ample revenge on Ernesto. He had, after all, taken over his entire circus, and for a long time had even adopted his son. Not only that, but Ernesto's first attempt to make a comeback after the tragic death of his wife had been curtailed when he'd come off stage to find his dressing room filled with piles of money he'd never seen before and a neat array of mementos from the Retired Police Dog Benevolent Fund. Seconds later, following a tip-off from You Know Who, officers had burst in, and that was that. Jail. Two years of toenail-clipping chess with Magwitch Intertextuality McDickens. Without winning even once.

For most people, that would have been revenge enough. But not Armitage Shank. He could never recover from the wound of Esmeralda choosing Ernesto over him, and felt that he would never be happy until Ernesto had been banished from circusry for ever. (The fact is, Armitage would never be happy whatever happened. He was not a happy person. He didn't even like being happy. But he was stuck with the idea that making Ernesto unhappy gave his life meaning.)♥

Armitage paced and twirled, twirled and paced, all night long. The one-handed twirl left him

---

♥Like many aggressive and angry people, Armitage was in fact very needy. He had never been loved. He'd never been loved because he was horrible. But, on the other hand, maybe he was horrible because he'd never been loved.

appearing rather lopsided by the time dawn began to glimmer through the misted-up caravan windows, but if you had seen him, before you noticed that half of his moustache was coiled into a spiral, you would have been struck by the gleam of devious cunning that was burning in his eyes, like two cauldrons of flaming Ribena.

Yes, Armitage had a plan! This time it was truly his most despicable plot ever! Hockney Marshes on 1st January was going to be in for a surprise. It was going to find itself playing host to something entirely unprecedented in the history of circus, criminality, vengefulness and general nasty behaviour. Armitage wasn't just going to steal Ernesto's money. That wouldn't be nearly enough to exact the revenge that was required. Armitage was going to go one step further. He was going to hit Ernesto where it would really hurt. He was going to steal his money and his audience.

Armitage picked up his phone (a mobile which, to Armitage's embarrassment, was already two months out of date), searched for a number, and dialled.

'Helloooooooo,' said Armitage in his pretending-not-to-be-a-revolting-human-being voice. 'Is that advertising sales for *Pointless Expensive Gadgets You Must Buy*? I'd like to place an ad. It should say, **"ROLL UP, ROLL UP!** A CIRCUS LEGEND RETURNS TO THE STAGE! ARMITAGE SHANK'S VERY EXTREME IMPOSSIBLE CIRCUS. FOR ONE NIGHT ONLY! 1ˢᵗ JANUARY! HOCKNEY MARSHES! **PREPARE TO BE REALLY AMAAAAAAAAZED!!!"** HAHAHAHAHAHAHAHAHA! . . . No, the cackle isn't part of it. That was just me cackling . . . No, thanks . . . Just cut the cackle! . . . OK. Bye . . . HAHAHAHAHAHAHAHAHA!'

Armitage was happy again. Ernesto Espadrille would finally get the comeuppance he'd been asking for. Armitage would finally show him the dismal fate that awaited if you went around being nice and popular and talented all the time, making people fall in love with you, and forgot more important things, like being wary and devious and suspicious.

Armitage stepped out of his caravan into the crisp dawn air. He hated fresh air – couldn't stand the stink of it – but nothing was going to dent his good mood this morning. The past couple of months had been the low point of his entire career but now, at last, he had a plan. He was on the up. He was back in the saddle. He was in the swing. It was time for revenge. It was time for a comeback.

FOUR

Hannah gets an unhygienic letter

POOR HANNAH. PLUCKY YOUNG HANNAH, who, along with Billy, had foiled Armitage's last plot, to rob Queenie Bombazine at the Oh, Wow! centre. Because of her efforts, Hannah had thought she might be taken up as Queenie's new trapeze protégée; she'd thought that her long-held dream of leaving her boring life and joining the circus might at last become a reality, but things hadn't worked out that way.

Queenie's show, it turned out, was a one-off.

She wasn't looking for a new star. All she'd wanted was to raise enough money to pay off her debts and build a couple of new bathrooms. The Oh, Wow! show had done the job, and Queenie had scurried straight back into retirement like a skinny-dipper sprinting for a towel, leaving Hannah with no option but to return home to her less-than-fascinating parents.■

But Hannah was not one to give up so easily on her dream. She'd been working on a plan of her own. She had been in training. In just a few years she'd be old enough to live wherever she wanted, with whoever she wanted, doing whatever she wanted – and if what she wanted was to fulfil her circus destiny, then right now was the time to get into training.

Hannah's real mother had been a trapeze artist, so that's where she began, except that trapeze artistry isn't something you can practise in a tiny

---

■ I had to work really hard there to avoid using the word 'boring'. Did you notice? It's very important to be polite about people behind their backs. But on the other hand it's also important to be interesting, and Hannah's parents were really, really dull.

bedroom. She had tried, rigging up a home-made swing from the pendant light, but that hadn't gone well, not for her, not for the light, and not for the plaster ceiling. Trapeze was out.

She'd also tried juggling, but every time she dropped something, her parents shouted up through the floor for her to stop thumping. This happened once every two seconds. So juggling was out.

She gave clowning a go, but it's very hard to be funny on your own, and almost impossible to tell whether or not the thing you think is funny actually is. Also, clowning on your own in a bedroom is strangely depressing. Clowning was definitely out.

But eventually she found the answer. Tightrope-walking, she discovered, could be rehearsed almost anywhere. Hannah had rigged up two ropes in her home, one from her bedpost to the door jamb, the other at a diagonal across the garden. After a long negotiation with her over-cautious, over-protective, over-anxious mother, a height of approximately twenty centimetres off the ground had been agreed for these ropes. Hannah found this deeply unsatisfying, so she had printed out some satellite photos which she put on the ground under the rope, to make her feel as if she was high in the sky, as a way of working on her fearlessness. Not that it needed much work. Fearlessness came easy to Hannah. Which is probably why her over-cautious, over-protective, over-anxious mother suffered from a nervous condition that made her left eye twitch whenever she heard a loud noise, and her right eye twitch when she heard a quiet one. If she saw Hannah climb anything, ride anything or jump off anything, both eyes twitched and her nostrils did a strange flarey thing like an angry horse.

Climbing things, riding things and jumping off things were Hannah's favourite activities.

Motherhood had not come easy to Hannah's mother. But then, as you probably remember, Hannah's mother was not Hannah's mother. She was her aunt. Her real mother was the trapeze supremo, Esmeralda Espadrille, whose trapezing days were now sadly over, on account of her being dead.✖

But back to the matter at hand. We find Hannah in the garden, on her tightrope, balancing on one leg with her eyes closed, her head tipped up, a stick on her chin, and a plate on the end of the stick, which she is trying to spin. Hannah's mother is watching out of the living room window, twitching both eyes and flaring her nostrils.

'She's a worry to me, that girl,' said Hannah's mother, whose name, as you probably won't remember, was Wanda.⚠

'I know, dear,' said Hannah's father, who was concentrating intently on his matchstick model of the Forth Rail Bridge.

'This is going to cause no end of trouble.'

'I know, dear.'

'She's going to get injured.'

'I know, dear.'

✖ If you're having trouble remembering who was responsible for her death, I'll give you a clue: it's a name that rhymes with Barmitage Bank.

⚠ Wanda, as it happens, is the Ancient Greek goddess of Health and Safety.

'Or worse.'

'I know, dear.'

'Are you listening to anything I'm saying?'

'I know, dear.'

'You're not, are you?'

'I know, dear.'

'This is pointless.'

'I know, dear.'

At this moment the letterbox flap flapped. Wanda hurried to the hall with some antiseptic wipes, since postmen are well known to have surprisingly dirty hands.

The letter on the doormat had brightly coloured edging – orange and blue and green and purple – and the paper of the envelope was yellow. The address was in red and bore Hannah's name.

Wanda picked up the suspicious item of post between finger and thumb and examined it closely. She did not like the look of this letter at all.

Hannah

This missive was distinctly, unmistakably, shamelessly . . . circussy.

Hannah was out in the garden practising plate-spinning tightrope tricks, so there was a moment when the letter could have been concealed, but the window of opportunity was too brief. In a flash, Hannah (who seemed to have some kind of radar for detecting interesting deliveries) was right there, at her mother's side, looking up at the unusual envelope.

'Wow!' she said. 'It's beautiful.'

'Gaudy, I'd say,' replied Wanda.

'Look! It's for me!'

Hannah took the letter without so much as a please or thank you or even the briefest dab with an antiseptic wipe, and ripped it open.

'UNBELIEVABLE!' she yelled. 'A COMEBACK SHOW! Ernesto and Billy are opening tomorrow, on Hockney Marshes, in a new Big Top. We've been sent VIP tickets for the opening night! Isn't that brilliant?'

'Brilliant' was not the word that immediately occurred to Wanda. Circuses were, frankly, not her scene. And she didn't like tents. Or crowds. Or Hockney Marshes. Or surprises, especially when they arrived on gaudy stationery. She'd never been to an opening night, but she didn't really like the sound of that, either. Billy, however, was Hannah's at-least-half-brother. And Ernesto . . . well . . . that was a *looooong* story, but he was very important to Hannah, too. So, despite her feelings about circuses, tents and opening nights, Wanda knew that declining the invitation wasn't an option.

In the interests of parental bonding, she decided to opt for enthusiasm. 'Er . . . wow?' she said. 'How lovely? We'll have to wrap up warm, because it'll be very draughty.'

Enthusiasm was not her forte.

'Isn't this just the most fantastic, fabulous, frazilliant letter you have EVER SEEN?' replied Hannah, to whom enthusiasm came a little more naturally.

'Er . . . frazilliant isn't a real word, but I can tell that you're attempting to express jollity and eagerness, which can be very healthy emotions in moderation. So, well done.'

'LET'S GET READY! LET'S PACK! LET'S DO IT NOW, NOW, NOW!'

Hannah sprinted up the stairs to her room, and the first thing she packed – before her clothes, before her toothbrush, before anything else – was her tightrope. Because Hannah knew this was much more than an opportunity to see her at-least-half-brother perform. Oh, yes. This was the chance she'd been waiting for. Now, at last, she was ready. She didn't know how she was going to make it happen but, one way or another, when she got herself in front of Ernesto Espadrille, she wasn't going to let him leave without giving her an audition. And after all the hours of practice she'd put in, she was confident she had enough tricks to impress him. This time, she'd find her way into the circus, where she knew she belonged.

Hannah had always known she was different – not an ordinary civilian like her parents – and now, at last, a real opportunity to break free and join the circus had arrived.

This was it! Hannah's moment had arrived!

FIVE

A touching reunion without touching

RE YOU READY?

I can put it off no longer.

It's time to plumb the depths of Shankiness. Time to delve to the very bottom of the cesspit of human nature. Time . . . for ZACHARY SHANK.

There he is! Just look at him! Flopped in a saggy old armchair, twirling his moustache, moaning and groaning and grumping and sulking.

'This is DISGUSTING!' he's yelling, holding a

mug at arm's length. 'When I ask for tea with five sugars, I want tea with five sugars. Not four sugars. Not six sugars. Not four and a half sugars. Not five and a half sugars. How many did you put in?'

'Five!' replied his apprentice, trainee, office runner and factotum Mungo Einstein (who was descended from a famous mathematician, but had sadly inherited not one single gene worth having).

'Five? Are you sure?'

'Yes. I counted them and everything,' said Mungo, who was on the brink of pointing out his impressive arithmetical ancestry.

'Which teaspoon did you use?'

'Just . . . a teaspoon. A normal one.'

'Which one?'

'The one with a sticker on it.'

'Did you read the sticker?'

'No. You told me to make you the tea as fast as I can, and reading a sticker would have slowed me down.'

'That sticker says, "DO NOT USE THIS TEASPOON FOR TEA-MAKING BECAUSE IT IS OF BELOW AVERAGE SIZE," you moron! This tea is revolting.'

'Sorry.'

'I should have known you were a moron from the moment you turned up seven hours late for your interview, covered from head to toe in sewage because you'd had a "small accident" on the way.'

'There was a missing manhole cover.'

'You're just lucky I don't pay you anything

because, if I did, this is the moment I'd sack you.'

'Sorry, guv. I'll make you another tea right away, with a different spoon.'❮

'Get Miss Ingperson to make it. She's the only one round here with any brains. Apart from me, obviously.'

Miss Ingperson was Zachary's secretary. He had kidnapped her several years earlier and nobody had wanted to pay the ransom because nobody liked her, but then it turned out that Miss Ingperson actually liked Zachary, which wasn't something that had ever happened before, because nobody ever liked him, either. Not long after that, they fell in love, so Zachary employed her as a secretary, which is what he did every time he fell in love. He was not a great romantic.

'Oh, it wasn't like this back in the good old days, when the old crew were around,' Zachary whinged. 'I tell you, those guys could have taught you a thing

---

❮ Insightful readers may have noticed a spoon theme emerging in this text. This often happens in great works of literature. Themes that is. Not spoons.

or two. Top bunch of lads they were, before they got banged up. Frankie Geezer, Chippy Barnet and Vince Hurtle – that was the best crew I ever had. Solid gold, they were. Don't make 'em like that any more, I'll tell you that for free. WHY ARE YOU STILL STANDING THERE? WHERE'S MY TEA?'

'Sorry.'

At this moment, something quite extraordinary happened. The door burst open, and who should enter but three men wearing mud-caked Grimwood Scrubs prison uniforms? None other than Frankie Geezer, Chippy Barnet and Vince Hurtle.

What are the chances of that? Eh?

Very low.

Verging on zero, in fact.

BUT IT HAPPENED!

Yes, it did.

'Frankie, is that you?' said Zachary, leaping up from his chair.

'It's me, guv.'

'Chippy?' said Zachary, striding towards the three men, filled with relief and joy, while at the same time wondering how to greet three long-lost friends who were at this point the filthiest human beings he had seen since Mungo Einstein's sewage pipe accident. A hug wasn't tempting. Even a handshake was kind of unappealing.

'The one and only,' replied Chippy, his huge toothy grin glinting whitely through the muck.

'Vince?'

'We escaped, boss! Dug ourselves out! Took us seven years, four months and nineteen days, but we did it!'

'We dun it!' affirmed Chippy, pointedly.

'Well, this calls for a celebration,' said Zachary. 'Big time. Miss Ingperson! Cups of tea all round! Large ones! And crack open a fresh packet of plain digestives!'

Zachary Shank was not a generous man.

'I missed you, fellas,' he continued, slumping back into his armchair. 'I missed you something rotten. Thought about you all the time, I did. Proper choked up, I was, when you boys went down.'

'We were pretty choked up, too,' said Vince. 'Twelve years, and all. That was my prime, that was. Ripped away from me. And for what?'

'Armed robbery,' said Zachary.

'No, "for what" as in, for what purpose? I mean, why would I do that to myself?'

'To get rich.'

'No – I just mean, what was the point? It was all a huge mistake, wasn't it?'

'Getting caught was,' said Zachary with a long, wheezy laugh, which the other three did not join.

'Hi, fellas,' said Miss Ingperson, entering with a tray of teacups and a small packet of Tesco Basics digestives.

'Tuck in, lads,' said Zachary. 'Have as many as you like. On me. Up to a maximum of two.'

'Thanks, boss,' said Frankie. 'It's great to be back.'

'Boss,' said Miss Ingperson, which is an unusual way to address the love of your life, but they were

an unusual couple. 'There's something you ought to know. I been getting calls. Somebody's putting something up on Hockney Marshes.'

'Hockney Marshes?'

'Yes, boss.'

'Putting something up?'

'Yes, boss.'

'But that's my manor! That's my back door! Nobody puts nothing up on Hockney Marshes without asking ME first!'

'Yes, boss. That's why I thought I should tell you.'

'Putting what up?' said Vince. 'What is it?'

'Apparently it's some kind of . . . tent.'

'A tent?' said Zachary. 'Oh, right. Like, a hippy or something. I thought you meant something big.'

'Two-man or three-man?' said Chippy.

'It is something big.'

'Four-man?' said Frankie. 'Family-size?'

'Bigger.'

'How big?' said Zachary, whose moustache was now twitching anxiously.

'People are saying it looks like it might be a . . . a . . . Big Top.'

'A BIG TOP?! A BIG TOP!! IN MY MANOR!!! HOW THE . . .? WHO THE . . .? WHAT THE . . .?'

If there was one thing Zachary hated – and there was way more than one, what with him being a Shank – but if there was one thing he hated even more than he hated all the other things that he hated, it was circuses. He loathed them. Could not stand them. Just the word 'circus' made him livid. The sight of a Big Top sent him apoplectic. The idea of one going up on his patch . . . that was too much.

There was no question of what he would do now. He wasn't just going to take it down. He wasn't just going to exact revenge. This meant war.

'There's one other thing,' said Miss Ingperson, her voice wavering with anxiety.

'What?'

'It's only a rumour.'

'What?'

'Some people are saying . . .'

'What?'

'That there's . . .'

'What?'

'Two of them. Bye.'

With that, Miss Ingperson ran out of the room.

Frankie, Chippie and Vince followed, making some excuse about needing a shower.

Steam doesn't really come out of people's ears. That only happens in cartoons. But if it did, at this point Zachary would have been boiling like a kettle.

Zachary was often angry. In fact, he was usually angry. Even when he was asleep, he slept angrily, tossing and turning, grinding his teeth, and occasionally biting chunks out of the duvet. But even for him this was something special. As soon as he stopped twitching and fuming, he was going to head straight out to Hockney Marshes and teach these ignorant circussers a lesson about how things worked in his manor.

'GRRRRRAAAAAARRRRR RRGHHHHHHHHHH!' yelled Zachary, which doesn't mean anything, but he felt better for getting it off his chest.

'GRRRRRAAAAAARRRRR RRGHHHHHHHHHHH!' he repeated, grinding his half-eaten digestive to crumbs in his fist, which might have made him feel better still, if it weren't for the fact that the waste of a half a biscuit made him even crosser.

As I'm sure you have already figured out, Zachary would soon be finding out that one of these Big Tops belonged to his brother.

Could it be that Zachary and Armitage have a long-cherished fondness for one another, and that Zachary's anti-circus rage will be overwhelmed by his delight at seeing his beloved sibling? Or can we expect, perhaps, rather the opposite?

I wonder . . .

 SIX

HONK HONK HOOT HOOT HUBBA HUBBA DING DONG!

AVE YOU GOT YOUR SEATBELT ON?' said Wanda.

'Yes, Mum,' replied Hannah.

'Is it securely fastened?'

'Yes, Mum.'

'Is the passenger airbag enabled?'

'Yes, Mum.'

'Is your headrest correctly positioned to avoid

whiplash in the event of a collision?'

'Yes, Mum.'

'Then let's go!' she said, checking both mirrors and her blind spot before slipping the car into first gear, indicating and pulling out.

This, Hannah suspected, was not going to be as exciting a journey as the mountain tandem rampage with Granny when they'd cycled to the Oh, Wow! centre, but Wanda had asked to come so Hannah couldn't exactly turn her down. Why she had asked, when it was obvious Wanda liked circuses as much as lamp-posts like dogs, was a mystery.

'You're probably wondering why I want to come,' said Wanda, accelerating the car gradually to her favoured speed of ten per cent below the speed limit.

'I was, actually. How did you know?'

'Oh, I always know what you're thinking,' said Wanda.

'You never know what I'm thinking.'

'No, I don't. You're right. But this time it was your face. You had a kind of why-does-she-even-want-to-come? expression.'

'Did I?'

'Yes – and I'll tell you why. It's because, as you get older, in order to maintain the maternal bond, it becomes increasingly important to feign an

interest in your child's hobbies.'

'Feign an interest?'

'Take an interest.'

'You said "feign",' said Hannah.

'No, I said "take".'

'You definitely said "feign".'

'I said take. I want to take more of an interest in your passion for tightrope-walking . . . even though I think it is literally the most foolish and ill-advised hobby any young girl could possibly adopt . . . and I'd like to support you in your efforts to learn more about it . . . while also perhaps teaching you that it would be a really good idea to just give the whole thing up for ever and never do it again and just burn that stupid rope and take up basket-weaving or something.'

'That's . . . very supportive,' replied Hannah.

'I know,' said Wanda. 'I got a book from the library called *Pretending to be Nice is Your Only*

Option When Your Kid is Going off the Rails. It's full of excellent advice.'

'I'm not going off the rails!'

'You're not going off the rails because you were never on the rails. You've always been . . . wayward. Like your mother. Your other mother. But I think I've learned how to combat it with the power of niceness, so maybe everything's going to be OK now.'

'Wayward?'

'Yes, dear. Unconventional.'

'Is that bad?'

'It's appalling. But I think we can work round it.'

The rest of the journey passed in silence. It had definitely been more fun travelling with Granny.

Hannah didn't mind, though. As long as they ended up at Hockney Marshes in good time for Billy and Ernesto's show, it didn't matter what

Wanda said to her. The silence meant she could focus better on thinking through the plan she had devised for her coming audition. Over and over it she went, visualising every move, imprinting every gesture as deeply as she could into her mind, like a pianist playing a piece so many times that eventually it feels as if the piano is playing you.

As always happened when Wanda was in charge of the itinerary, they arrived roughly three hours early.[1] Which was perfect timing for Hannah's plan.

Before Wanda had even finished parking (which always took a while, on account of her insistence on being exactly parallel to the kerb and equidistant from adjacent vehicles), Hannah had leaped out of the car and run across Hockney Marshes in the direction of a certain camel.

Narcissus greeted her with a kiss on the cheek, which was a sensation akin to have having your

---

[1] I.e., every time they went anywhere

face shoved into a stinking, frothy puddle of taramasalata, but Hannah knew how special it was to receive this kind of affection from a camel (and a notoriously aloof one, at that) so she accepted the kiss graciously. Then she wiped her face. There are limits.

Billy appeared moments later, wielding a sledgehammer. At the sight of his at-least-half-

sister he dropped the hammer and ran into her arms.

'Oh, it's so good to see you again!' they both said, at exactly the same time.

'We just said the same thing,' they both added, at exactly the same time.

'This is weird,' they said, in unison.

'We have to stop,' said Hannah and Billy, precisely together.

'You stop first,' said Billy and Hannah.

'No, you,' said Hannah and Billy.

'HANNAH!' came another voice, mercifully breaking the weird spell of synchronised speaking. It was Ernesto, emerging at a run from the saggy half-put-up Big Top.

More hugs.

At this point, Wanda appeared.

'Oh, it is SOOOOOOO lovely to meet you at last,' said Ernesto, lifting Wanda off her feet in

---

This killed a worm, who had just poked her head above ground to see if it was raining. Sadly for the worm, it was raining sledgehammers. One sledgehammer, anyway, but if you're in the wrong place, one is enough. It's hard being a worm.

another powerful embrace.

'Put me down,' said Wanda, which wasn't the greeting she'd had in mind for Ernesto, but she really didn't like hugging strangers, even if they had married her sister.

Ernesto put her down.

'I mean to say, it's lovely to meet you, too,' said Wanda. 'I've heard so much about you. All of it . . . interesting.'

'Great!' said Ernesto, who was at this moment struggling to comprehend how this woman could be the twin sister of his charismatic, captivating, cool, classy and compelling wife, without apparently having a single thing in common with her. Apart from the ears. He definitely recognised the shape of those ears.⁹

'What on earth is that?' yelled Hannah, pointing not at Wanda's ears, but at a vehicle that was driving at speed across the grass of Hockney

---

⁹ Wanda
⁹ Wendy/Esmerelda

Marshes. It was a lorry. An unmistakably enormous lorry that looked very familiar.

On the side, it said

SHANK'S IMPOSSIBLE CIRCUS
VERY ↗
EXTREME

The enormous lorry roared towards them, dazzling Hannah with the light of seventeen headlamps on full beam.

'HONK HONK HOOT HOOT HUBBA HUBBA DING DONG!' said the enormous lorry, which was in possession of a very flashy horn.

The lorry came to a halt right in front of them, its brakes letting out a long sigh like a deflating hovercraft. The driver door swung open, and out poked a long limb encased in a preposterously tight trouser leg. Then another one, in matching attire. Then another one.

No, I've miscounted. He still had only two legs. But Armitage Shank was just as hideous as ever, all the more so for the gruesome mirthless grin that was smeared across his features as he leaped down from his enormous lorry.

'Well, helloooooooo,' he said. 'Fancy meeting you here! What a coincidence!'

'Why are you here?' said Ernesto. 'What are you up to, Shank?'

'Just plying my humble trade. Putting on a show.'

'Where?'

'Here. Goodness – is that droopy heap of canvas your Big Top? Or should I say Small Top? H a h a h a h a h a H A H A H A H A H A HAHAHAHAhahahaha!'

'You're putting on a show here?' said Ernesto. 'Now?'

'I am,' sneered Armitage. 'Fancy that! Looks like

we're going head to head! Good luck! Or should I say, break a leg! HahahahahahHAHAHA HAHAHAHAHAhahaha!'

'Why is that funny?' asked Billy.

'That wasn't a laugh. It was a cackle. Did I teach you nothing? All those years I wasted on you! The ingratitude! How sharper than a serpent's tongue . . . etc. . . . something . . . ungrateful child.'

'What?'

'That's Shakespeare, you know. He and I have a lot in common. I was always too good for you, Billy. I'm better off without you. And as for you! What are you doing here?' he snarled, in the direction of Hannah. 'It's never a good sign when you turn up.'

'I could say the same about you,' retorted Hannah.

'Well, I could say the same about you.'

'That doesn't mean anything.'

'Neither does that,' said Armitage.

'What are you talking about?' said Hannah, Billy, Ernesto and Wanda.

'JUST YOU WAIT AND SEE! You may have stolen half my troupe, Ernesto so-called Espadrille, but there's one thing you'll never steal. My talent. And my ingenuity. Two things. And you'll never have either of them. So there. WATCH AND LEARN! Because you've got a surprise coming. And even me telling you that you've got a surprise coming won't make the surprise any less surprising when it comes – THAT'S HOW SURPRISING IT IS. HAHAHAHAHAHA!'

With that, Armitage climbed back into his enormous lorry and drove off, belching out a thick cloud of diesel fumes (the lorry, that is, not Armitage – who did have bad breath, but not that bad).

He had barely driven ten metres before he parked and began to unload his Big Top, which was significantly smarter, and newer, and bigger, than Ernesto's.

Right behind the enormous lorry was a small (and very French) car, driven by Irrrrena, towing a caravan, on top of which a small, muscly (and very French) man was sitting, fully oiled, in a deck chair, waxing his moustache.

'Who was that awful person?' asked Wanda.

'This is fishy,' said Billy. 'Very fishy.'

'Why is he putting on a circus right next to your circus?' she added.

'Because he's up to something,' replied Hannah.

'And why are his trousers so tight?'

'Now that really is a mystery,' said Ernesto.

SEVEN

Joy of joys, rapture of raptures

HANNAH, AS YOU WILL REMEMBER, had a plan. She didn't just want to watch Ernesto's Extreme Extravaganza; she wanted to be in it. For this to be even remotely possible, she had to show off her tightrope-walking skills as soon as possible. It would be no good performing twenty centimetres off the ground, either. She'd have to demonstrate the real thing.

But if she wanted to do any proper tightrope-walking, first she'd have to get rid of her mother.

She pondered for a while, then a naughty idea suddenly streaked naked across her brain, shouting, 'WOO-HOO! I'M REALLY NAUGHTY! WHERE ARE MY CLOTHES? CHASE ME, CHASE ME!'

Wild and cheeky thoughts often did this in Hannah's brain, and she usually ignored them, but on this occasion she decided to go for it.

'Mum,' said Hannah, springing into action. 'I want you to meet someone. He's called Narcissus. He's the most amazing camel you'll ever meet.'

'Is he clean?'

'Clean enough.'

Hannah led Wanda to Narcissus' cage, picking up a bucket of taramasalata from Billy's caravan on the way.

'Do we really have to go in? What if I'm allergic to camel hair?'

'Just come and give him a stroke. He's lovely.'

Narcissus gazed out at Wanda sceptically. He lifted one lip, showing off a row of pondweed-coloured teeth. A waft of semi-digested-taramasalata gas billowed out. This was not a greeting Wanda had experienced before.

'Can't I stroke him through the bars?'

'Just come in. He's lovely.'

Wanda gingerly stepped into the cage. She gingerly, at Hannah's insistence, gave him a pat. With no less ginger than before, she gave him a small stroke. Still in the manner of a gnarled but flavoursome root vegetable, she opened the bucket of taramasalata and held it out. Narcissus eyed Wanda through his long and beautiful eyelashes, then extended his long and not very beautiful tongue towards the pink paste. He lapped and slurped, sometimes smacking his lips to keep his bristles taramasalata-free. All the while, he maintained eye contact with Wanda, which she found more than a little unnerving.

'Do you like him?' asked Hannah.

'I think this is one of the most unpleasant experiences I've ever had,' replied Wanda, which wasn't the response Hannah was hoping for.

'Stay there,' she said. 'Don't move.'

This is when Hannah put into action her naughty-mind-streak idea, slipping out of the cage and locking the door behind her.

'Hannah? Hannah! HANNAH! What are you doing?'

'Just popping out for a second. Don't let go of the bucket.'

'Where are you going? Let me out!'

'I'm not going anywhere. Just stay put.'

'Of course I'll stay put! You've locked me in! Let me out right now!'

'Sorry, I can't. There's something I have to do.'

'What could you possibly have to do that's more

important than freeing your mother from imprisonment with a camel?'

'An audition.'

'You're delirious. Let me out.'

'I can't. You'd interfere. You'd nag and tell me off and warn me to be careful every five seconds. You have to stay in there. Not for long. You'll be fine. Narcissus is perfectly safe as long as you don't annoy him and give him plenty of taramasalata.'

'Are you saying you locked me in here on purpose?'

'Sort of.'

'This is completely unacceptable!'

'I'll be back soon. Have fun.'

'Fun? This cage is neither safe nor healthy! NEITHER!'

Hannah immediately rigged up her tightrope from the top of Narcissus' cage to the roof of a caravan, while Billy rushed around the site, grabbing Ernesto, Delia de la Doolah and Vonda van der Venda, Chancey Bris, Bellagio Spigot, Hank, Frank, Jesse, Halle Tosis, Mitzi Schnitzel and the Caapaak family (Empti, Mülti-Störi, Shortstaï, Longstaï and Payandisplaï). Soon, the whole troupe had assembled to see Hannah's audition.

None of them knew it was an audition. They thought it was just some girl showing off a few amateurish skills, but Billy had physically dragged every one of them to a row of chairs he'd set up in front of the tightrope, so they had little choice but to watch. They weren't expecting to enjoy themselves, and they certainly weren't expecting to be impressed by this frankly rather ordinary-looking girl. This left them quite unprepared for Hannah's display.

She tightrope-walked very nicely, of course, which came as no huge surprise, but when she began to cartwheel, somersault, back-flip, front-flip and side-flip, her audience sat up.

Wanda was not so impressed. She had only a restricted view from inside Narcissus' cage, but she kept up a constant commentary on Hannah's show along the lines of, 'What on earth do you think you're doing up there? Get down! Get down, right now! No! Not a back-flip! Please, not a back-flip! Where's your safety harness? Those aren't . . . surely you're not going to juggle on the . . . the . . . NO! Don't light them! What are you doing? That's very unsafe! That is a naked flame! Three of them! You don't have a permit for that! You're going to burn your hands! Your hair could catch fire! Is that . . .?

I hope you're not going to ... You take that blindfold off right now, young lady, or I'll ... I'll ... Put down those plates! At once! Are you listening to me? I happen to have considerable expertise in the field of health and safety, and if you think it's advisable to spin plates while juggling fire, blindfolded on a high wire, you've got another thing coming, my girl!

You just ... STOP THAT AT ONCE!'

Only when Narcissus delivered a modest but well-aimed quantity of camel goo onto Wanda's cheek did she finally go quiet. Not because she now accepted that Hannah knew what she was doing, or because she could tolerate being spat on by a dromedary, but because she fainted.

Her commentary would no longer have been audible anyway, because Hannah had just pulled off her final stunt, and a deluge of clapping, stamping and cheering was rising from Hockney Marshes.

Not far away, a man with a droopy moustache and alarmingly tight trousers, leaning against an enormous lorry, gave three small claps – possibly sarcastic, possibly not.

'Not bad,' he said. 'Not good,' he added. 'But not bad.'

Hannah, meanwhile, was surrounded by congratulators, huggers, hand-shakers and back-slappers. Ernesto was the first to tell her how wowed he was by her talents, but he was also the first to retreat, rapidly thinking through his running order to find a place where he could fit Hannah into his show.

When the bustle and excitement had subsided, Hannah felt Ernesto's strong hand grip her shoulder.

'I've found a spot,' he said. 'In the second half.'

'For . . . you mean . . .?' Hannah hardly dared think, let alone say, the words that were on the tip of her lips.

'You're ready. I'd like you to perform in my circus.'

Joy of joys, rapture of raptures, thrill of thrills, etc. of et ceteras – Hannah's greatest dream had at last come true. She could hardly believe her ears. Or her eyes. Or her nose.

'Really?' she said.

'Really. You're good. You've got something. When you were up there it reminded me of . . .'

Ernesto's voice tailed away. His eyes glistened.

'My real mum? Esmeralda Espadrille?'

Ernesto nodded. A heavy, velvety silence settled over them.

'You'll have a safety net,' he said, eventually. 'You have to promise me you'll never perform without a safety net.'

'I won't.'

This promise reminded her of her other mother. Hannah hadn't yet looked to see why Wanda's barrage of objections had stopped halfway through her performance. The dual snore emitted by an unconscious Wanda and a snoozing Narcissus gave her the explanation. Narcissus seemed to have decided that Wanda's stomach made a perfect pillow, and he was drooling contentedly onto this resting place as he dozed.

'Welcome to the troupe,' said Ernesto, extending a leathery palm towards Hannah.

She reached out and shook his hand, her heart kabooming against her ribs like a gorilla trapped under a xylophone. This was the happiest moment of Hannah's entire life.

Meanwhile, not far away – but a little further away than a moment ago – another man with another droopy moustache and strangely loose tracksuit trousers (who bore a striking resemblance to the first droopy-moustached man in the strangely tight ringmaster trousers) was leaning against a white van. He was looking angry. Which is how he looked all the time. But he was also looking puzzled.

'Flaming 'eck!' he said. 'There is two of them. Two Big Tops. Right next door to each other. And is that? . . . It can't be! . . . No way! . . . Blow me down!

It is! . . . That's my bleedin' brother!'

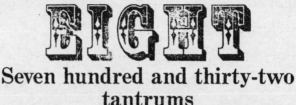

EIGHT

Seven hundred and thirty-two tantrums

LET US GO BACK FOR A MOMENT TO WHEN Armitage was in short (rather than tight) trousers. A little scamp, he was. A proper tearaway. Look – there he is, crouched in the dirt, pulling the legs off a spider. And there's Zachary, perched in a nearby tree, preparing to throw fistfuls of conkers at his brother's head. Ah, family life. How sweet!

But all was not well in the Shank household. A hideous rivalry had already begun, which was to cloud the lives of the Shank twins for decades to come. For Armitage's fifth birthday he'd been given the best present of his life: a toy vehicle – a tiny enormous lorry. This tiny enormous lorry was his pride and joy. He loved that tiny enormous lorry.

But one day, when Zachary was off school with a cold (which Armitage would always insist was faked) he 'borrowed' the tiny enormous lorry from the top-secret hiding place where Armitage always stashed it.

When Armitage returned from school, he found the tiny enormous lorry back in its hiding place, broken.

He threw a tantrum. Which was not an unusual occurrence. As you know, he still throws tantrums to this day.

But obviously not secret enough.

Armitage's mother did what she usually did when he threw a tantrum. She caved in and bought him another one.

Which Zachary also 'borrowed'.

And broke.

Leading to another tantrum.

And another tiny enormous lorry.

And another not-secret-enough hiding place.

'Borrowed'.

Broke.

Tantrum.

New tiny enormous lorry.

And so on, until Armitage and Zachary's mother finally said, 'That's it! I've had enough! No more tiny enormous lorries. I'm sick of it.'

'BUT HE BROKE IT! IT WASN'T MEEEEEE! IT'S NOT FAAAAIIIIIIIIR! HE KEEPS STEALING THEM! HE'S BREAKING THEM ON PURPOSE. IT'S NOT FAAAIIIIIIRRR! WAAAA WAAA

WAAAA NOT FAIR NOT FAIR NOT FAIR NOT FAIR! NOT FAIR!'

So she brought Armitage another tiny enormous lorry.

Which Zachary broke.

After seven hundred and thirty-two lorries, and seven hundred and thirty-two tantrums, Armitage's mother finally stood up to him. There were to be no more tiny enormous lorries.

So then Armitage 'got a cold', 'borrowed' everything Zachary owned, took it all out into the garden, and lit a huge, satisfying and extremely naughty bonfire.

From then on, relations between the two brothers deteriorated.

Zachary and Armitage should have made very good siblings. They should have got on wonderfully. After all, they had so much in common: deceit, moodiness, dishonesty, treachery, meanness,

selfishness, disloyalty – they were a perfect match. Except things didn't turn out that way.

They loathed one another.

So when Zachary saw his brother and his Big Top and his enormous enormous lorry parked right in the middle of Hockney Marshes, next to another Big Top he couldn't identify, he concluded this was a deliberate provocation. To which there was only one response.

Revenge!

But Zachary didn't just plan to do him over. Oh, no. That wouldn't be nearly good enough. He wanted to really hit Armitage where it hurt, and stealing his cash was only half the job. Zachary knew Armitage better than anyone, and he knew there was one thing almost as precious to Armitage as money. His audience.

If Zachary really wanted to kipper him, he had to nick both. If he could pull that off, there would be no doubt left in anyone's mind as to who was Brother Number One.

How, you might wonder, can you steal an audience? In particular, how can you steal the audience of a show that has been put on for the specific purpose of stealing the audience of another show? And how can you do this without confusing the bejeezus out of anyone attempting to follow what is going on?

Well, Zachary had a pretty good idea that Armitage would be up to something. He knew Shank's Impossible Circus was more than just a circus, and that Armitage was bound to be sneaking off at some point during the show to make mischief of one kind or another. Which, of course, would create a rather enticing window of opportunity for a brother of almost identical appearance: a brother who could very easily slip into a pair of tight trousers, a billowy shirt and a red tailcoat, and could then quite easily go on stage in the guise of his brother and . . . well . . . he hadn't quite decided what he'd do just yet, but the goal was simple. To wreak havoc!

Zachary took out his phone and sent an urgent text to Frankie Geezer, Chippy Barnet and Vince Hurtle:

YOU BOYS ARE BACK IN BUSINESS!
I GOT A JOB FOR YOU. HOCKNEY MARSHES.
NOW. IT'S GONNA BE A BIG ONE.

Vince almost texted back, taking issue with his use of the word 'gonna', but decided against it.

'A big one,' said Frankie, to Chippy and Vince. 'I don't know about that. I was thinking of going straight.'

'You couldn't go straight if you moved into a monastery,' snapped Chippy, who was staring intently into the mirror, working on his hairstyle, which consisted of eight strands of hair, all of them growing from just above his left ear, carefully combed across his skull to the other side. In high winds, the eight hairs stood straight up, which made him look as if a skydiving octopus had landed on the side of his head. Chippy Barnet usually stayed home on windy days.

'I could!' said Frankie. 'But a little something to get me started might help. Maybe I'll just do this one, then retrain as a potter. I'd like to make coffee cups.'

'Make coffee cups? Hah! That's a mug's game,' said Chippy, which is such a bad joke this chapter has to end right here before things get any worse.▢

▢ If you don't know what 'a mug's game' means, count yourself lucky, because you have been spared a truly attrocious gag. It's a Cockney phrase meaning a foolish or pointless enterprise. There. Now you know. You were better off before, weren't you?

The giant knicker puppy quicksand illusion

YOU'RE PROBABLY WORRIED ABOUT Wanda, aren't you? Passed out, locked in a cage with a hungry camel. Or maybe you don't really care. She is kind of annoying.

Well, worried or not, you will be pleased/disappointed✖ to hear that she came round not in the hairy, foetid embrace of a flatulent dromedary with a fondness for Greek dips, but in Mitzi Schnitzel's comfortable, cosy, calm, congenial caravan.

✖ Delete as appropriate

This wasn't quite as soothing an experience as you might think, since Mitzi's taste in interior decor was eccentric, verging on alarming. Her home was one of those arched gypsy caravans with steps up to the door, and was painted all over with marigolds and daisies. More than once, in summer time, she had parked in a meadow and completely lost the entire caravan, so effectively was it camouflaged.

Inside, her decorative eccentricity had really blossomed. Mitzi loved frills and fripperies and draperies and tassels and doilies. Every single surface of the walls, floor, windows and ceiling was given over to some kind of lacy, dangly decoration.

Wanda's first thought when she woke up was, 'Stalactites! I'm in a cave! Made of lace? It's not a cave! I'm in a huge pair of frilly knickers! But that's not possible! Where am I? I've gone mad! I'm hallucinating giant underwear!'

'Cup of tea for you, dear?' said Mitzi. 'It's my own blackberry, ginseng and arnica blend. Perfect for a fright.'

'Am I inside a huge pair of knickers?' replied Wanda, which is what people often said in Mitzi's caravan, so she wasn't too offended.

'No, dear, you're in an authentic, traditional caravan fashioned from original timber, hand-assembled by local artisans on a vegan diet.'

'Does it meet with approved fire regulations?' said Wanda, who was never off duty. Health and safety was not just her career, it was a true passion. This is often said about the world's greatest artists; less often about the world's greatest health and safety officers.

'I have no idea,' said Mitzi, 'and I don't even care.'

Already, they weren't getting on. Wanda simply

never clicked with circus folk. Then a new terror overtook her.

'I'm in a quicksand!' she shrieked. 'I'm drowning! It's sucking me under!'

'No, dear. Don't worry,' replied Mitzi. 'That's just what it feels like to have your feet licked by seventeen puppies.'

Wanda looked down. Seventeen puppies were licking her feet.

She did not like this. Not one little bit. Seventeen wet, leathery little tongues tickling between her toes. This was a hygiene catastrophe.

'Where are my shoes and socks?' she snapped.

'I treated you to a spot of reflexology while you were out cold. Your chakras were screaming out for realignment.'

Wanda stared at Mitzi blankly. 'I'm afraid I don't understand a single word of what you just said,' she replied, 'but I hope it doesn't mean you touched

---

✳ Some people believe chakras are invisible channels of energy that run through the human body. Other people think that's a load of old phooey. Wanda, as you can probably guess, was firmly in the phooey camp.

my feet.'

Mitzi stared back, even more blankly. This conversation wasn't going well.

Wanda raised her legs off the ground, crossed them safely out of puppy range, and took a sip of tea. It tasted of compost, but out of politeness she pretended to like it.

'Nice tea,' she said, hauling her lips from a pucker of revulsion into what she hoped resembled a smile. 'Refreshing.'

'I'll tip it away if you hate it,' replied Mitzi.

Wanda wasn't very good at pretending.

'Thanks,' Wanda replied, handing back the cup (which was so frilly and lacy it looked less like a cup than . . . well . . . a tiny pair of knickers) and saucer (which had all the solidity and heft of a spider's web) and teaspoon (which was roughly the size of a matchstick).

Mitzi hadn't really expected Wanda to hand

🥄 Another spoon! Mmmm. Very profound.

back the tea with such haste, but she tried her best to conceal her hurt feelings.

These two were not destined to be pals. An awkward silence descended.

Another awkward silence rose up through the floorboards.

Then one more came in through the window and another one down the filigree cast-iron chimney.

Four silences in a row is pretty much the maximum before medical help is required. Mitzi decided to try one last attempt at conversation.

'Would you like to see my collection of porcelain unicorns?' she asked.

'No,' replied Wanda. 'Not today, thanks.' She wasn't in the mood for porcelain unicorns. She had never been in the mood for porcelain unicorns, and never would be.

Three more silences seeped into the room: a

chilly one through the keyhole, a frosty one from the fridge, and a smelly one from under the toilet door.

Three quarters of the way into silence number eight, Hannah burst in.

'I passed the audition! I passed the audition!' she yelled. 'Ernesto is giving me a slot in the show! I've made it! I've gone circus! I'm officially a tightrope-walker! A real one!'

This news was almost as unwelcome to Wanda as puppy-tongue reflexology.

Mitzi leaped up and gave Hannah a huge hug. 'That's wonderful!' she said. 'You deserve it. Your audition was brilliant.'

Wanda roused herself and realised this is what she should have said, what with being Hannah's mother and all. She had almost forgotten her *Pretending to be Nice is Your Only Option When Your Kid is Going off the Rails* regimen.

'That's what I was going to say,' said Wanda, a little unconvincingly. 'But the law states that you have to be sixteen to undertake paid employment. Never mind. It's not long to wait.'

'I don't want to be paid.'

'It's only four years. It'll give you more time to practise.'

'Mum – I have to do it.'

'We'll see about that.'

'You can't stop me!'

'Oh, yes I can.'

'Mum! Please! Pleasepleasepleeeeeeeeeeeaaaaa aaaaaaase!'

'I'd love you to take part, Hannah, I really would, if it was safe. But it isn't. Perhaps they'll let you tear the tickets or something like that.'

'Tear the tickets?'

'Paper cuts are a risk, of course, but as long as you're careful . . . '

'MUM! YOU DON'T UNDERSTAND!'

'I understand perfectly well. Why do you think tightropes are always so high off the ground?'

'Because . . . because it's more exciting.'

'Exactly. The only reason people pay to watch tightrope-walking is because they're excited by the idea that the performer might fall off and get hurt. It's ghoulish.'

'No! They want to watch because it's beautiful and inspiring and magical!'

'Piffle! I won't let you do it. It's against all my principles.'

'Which principles?'

'Two principles I hold very dear. Health and safety. Imagine what my colleagues would say if—'

Before Wanda could elaborate on the professional embarrassment attached to having her daughter join the circus as a tightrope-walker, she was interrupted by an unexpected knock at the door. Then two more, louder and angrier than the first one, though less unexpected.

'Come in,' said Mitzi, warily. 'It's open. Mind your head on the flamboyant fandango of frills, fripperies and fancies.'

And who was it?

Who?

(This is how you build tension. You ask pointless questions.)

Who, you ask?

At the door?

Knocking?

But not coming in for a bit?

(It gets kind of annoying after a while.)

Knocking?

At the door?

(Maybe I should stop now.)

Are you tense enough?

Are you ready?

Now?

(I can't stop. I don't know what's happened to me.)

Why is this happening?

Why am I stuck asking pointless questions?

How long is this going to last?

OK, OK! Enough!

I'll tell you who it was.

Right now.

Immediately.

In the next paragraph.

Now I'm making pointless statements.

Which makes a nice change.

ENOUGH!

OK.

This is the moment.

Now.

It was . . .

. . . GRANNY!

Waving her stick!

With an unusually determined look on her face.

Without so much as a hello, or a 'how do you do?', or a 'would you like a mint humbug?', Granny marched towards Wanda, pinioned her with a mesmerising stare, and spoke in a voice so steely you could have used it to rivet a bridge. 'You listen here, my girl,' she said. 'I struggled my whole life to bring you and your sister up, and you were very different girls with very different needs, but the most important thing you need to know as a parent is that whatever you might want for your children, they are individuals and they have their own needs and desires. I've known Hannah here since she was a baby and I've always known that she's circus! She just is! It's who she is and it's in the blood and there's nothing you or Hannah or anyone can do about it so we all just have to stand back and let her be the person she wants to be and at the moment that is a tightrope-walker. It's so obvious it's like a plank of

w   o   o   d

whacking us
all   in   the
face   and   if
you stand in her
way you'll just make
her   miserable   and
disappointed   and
angry   and   more
determined   to   go

ahead and do it anyway. Ernesto's a good man. He'll give her a safety net and you might not like it but she just has to go up on that tightrope this evening and perform. No ifs, no buts, no quibbles, no HEALTH AND SAFETY! And that's that. Got it? And if I hear one word of complaint, you'll be going to bed early with no supper. OK? Now I'm halfway through a very exciting episode of *Celebrities You've Never Heard of Strictly Baking Cakes on Ice in the Jungle* so I don't have time for any objections, cheek or backchat. That's all I have to say. Goodbye.'

Granny turned, gave Hannah a secret wink, and left, miraculously swerving between every tassel, frippery and frill without disturbing a single one.

And that was how Hannah came to make her circus debut.

Don't fall, Hannah, don't fall!

DRUM ROLL, PLEASE.

Darkness.

Spotlight.

Trumpet fanfare.

Whipcrack, whipcrack.

Applause.

And then . . .

Hannah was watching from the wings as Ernesto strode onto the stage in his ringmaster's outfit – top hat, crimson tailcoat, billowy shirt, tight (but not too tight) black trousers, and shoes so dark and shiny they positively glistened. My, he looked fine.

Hannah had never been more excited. The whole show drifted past her in a blur of delight and terror, nerves fluttering and twitching in her stomach. She barely took in Delia de la Doolah and Vonda van der Venda's contortionist knitting routine, and Chancey Bris's knife-throwing hardly sank in, either. Bellagio Spigot looked good, and the gasps from the audience were unmissable, but Hannah didn't hear a word he said. Only when a stray custard pie flew off stage and almost hit her in the face did she even really notice that Hank and Frank were in the ring.

The second half went even faster: Jesse, Halle Tosis and Mitzi Schnitzel each appearing to be on stage for only seconds each, and even though the sound of the Caapaaks' motorbike routine was deafening, this was the act that went by fastest of all, because Hannah's head was entirely filled with one thought, 'I'm next, I'm next, I'm next, I'm next,' which pounded round and round her skull even faster than those Finnish motorbikes.

Then it was time.

The tightrope was up. The safety net was in place.

Hannah could see Wanda in the front row, mouth open, hands over her eyes. But that wasn't important right now. At this moment, Hannah wasn't a daughter. She was a performer.

Hannah strode out and took a bow. As she straightened and looked up at the audience for the first time, an extraordinary sensation flowed through her body, starting in her heart and pulsing outwards through her veins, until it tingled in every part of her, right to her fingertips. For an instant she couldn't identify the feeling, then she realised it was the sensation of being perfectly, completely, utterly happy. This was her place. At long last, she was where she belonged.

Hannah spun on her heel and walked – no, pranced – without even intending to prance – it just seemed to happen on its own – to the rope ladder that led up to her tightrope. Time seemed to be charging ahead at a bewildering pace, while also moving with such precision and clarity that everything seemed to be in slow motion. Hannah's mind was now just a beam of pure, intense focus on the tightrope ahead of her.

Billy, at this point, was more nervous than Hannah. Even Narcissus, at his side, was nervous, which wasn't a sensation he'd ever had before.

'Haphuphuphuphkaglerp,' said Narcissus, which was his way of saying, 'I know you don't realise you're even doing it, but could you please stop pulling the hairs out of my neck.'

Billy was entirely lost in the sight of his at-least-half-sister's performance. Her audition had been good, but this was better. Billy could see, immediately, that Hannah was the real thing. If you are true circus, something happens when you're in front of a crowd that lifts you to a new level. Hannah was soaring. Every single trick and twirl and twist and leap was timed to perfection, not just for maximum beauty, but in tandem with the audience. She was playing their emotions like a musician plucking a harp: building and releasing tension, worrying then reassuring them, frightening then wowing them. This girl was special. If she was a civilian, Narcissus was a caterpillar.

Just as Hannah was reaching the climax of her act, with flaming torches flying up and down from both hands while a plate spun above her chin, there was an enormous bang, followed by a loud metallic clatter, followed by an astonished howl. It was a sound resembling an explosion, a safe door flying off its hinges, and a howl of bewildered dismay.

The sudden noise made everyone in the Big Top jump, which isn't much of a problem when you're sitting down, but is more serious when you are juggling on a tightrope.

Hannah wobbled. She dropped one of her torches, her body tipping one way and another, then found her balance again, focusing her gaze directly ahead of her. But at the edge of her vision, she couldn't miss the sight of that burning torch swivelling down through the air and coming to rest with a soft bounce on the safety net. The flame seemed to die for a second, then with a small crackle a circle of fire spread outwards. This only lasted a few seconds, but it left behind a hole in the net – a hole big enough for a young girl to fall clean through – directly below her.

Hannah began to wobble again, both arms flailing, and dropped her plate, which plunged to

the ground, through the hole in the net, shattering into a hundred pieces.✣

A moment ago, balancing on this tightrope seemed like the easiest thing in the world. Now Hannah was stricken by the idea that she couldn't sustain it a second longer. Perfect balance was as much a feat of the mind as the body, and her mind had lost its equilibrium.

She tried not to think about what happened to her mother. Her birth mother. But, of course, trying not to think about what happened to her mother was thinking about what happened to her mother. (Hannah's mother, you will remember, was a trapeze artist who would have still been alive if, during one particular performance in New Zealand, many years earlier, there had been a safety net.)

Hannah's body began to sway and tip.

Wanda screamed.

Billy pulled out a fistful of camel hair.

✣ Yes, a hundred. Yes, I counted them. Well, it looked like a hundred. Ish. OK, seven pieces. But a hundred sounds better.

Narcissus let out an anxious and fishy burp.

Don't fall, Hannah, don't fall!

But . . .

ELEVEN

Armitage's unsurprising surprise is interrupted by a surprisingly smelly surprise

BEFORE I TELL YOU WHAT HAPPENED to Hannah, I'm going to have to go back a little to explain the noise that distracted her.

Some of you may have guessed already.

Some of you probably have no idea.

Some of you might have dozed off.

If so, WAKE UP! Because Armitage is a-thieving again. Or trying to.

His first theft of the day was of Ernesto's

audience. As ticket-holders, circus fans and passers-by wandered across Hockney Marshes towards the two Big Tops, Armitage positioned himself directly in front of the Ernesto Espadrille box office, holding a loudhailer.

'**ROLL UP, ROLL UP,**' he shouted. '**A CIRCUS LEGEND RETURNS TO THE STAGE! ARMITAGE SHANK'S VERY EXTREME IMPOSSIBLE CIRCUS. FOR ONE NIGHT ONLY! PREPARE TO BE REALLY AMAAAAAAAAZED!!! DON'T BUY TICKETS HERE. THIS SHOW'S RUBBISH AND IS ROUGHLY A HALF TO A THIRD AS EXTREME AS MINE AND ONLY A QUARTER AS AMAZING. IF YOU WANT TO BE AMAAAAAAAAZED, GO NEXT DOOR. ROLL UP, ROLL UP!**'

Hannah and Billy tried to stop him, telling people it was all lies, but Armitage drowned them out with his loudhailer.

**'LOOK! CHILD PERFORMERS!
EXPLOITATION OF MINORS! IF YOU WANT
TO SEE CRUELTY TOWARDS CHILDREN,
THIS IS THE PLACE, OTHERWISE IT'S
SHANK'S VERY EXTREME IMPOSSIBLE
CIRCUS YOU WANT. RIGHT NEXT DOOR.
LOOK AT THESE POOR WAIFS! SEE THEIR
MISERY! ALL THEY WANT IS A SAFE HOME
AND A GOOD STURDY PAIR OF SHOES
LIKE ANY OTHER CHILD. ISN'T IT
HEARTBREAKING?'**

It was Narcissus who finally put a stop to him,

with a carefully aimed projectile of camel goo, right into the loudhailer, after which all Armitage could manage was, 'ROglogglegloggleLL UP, RObobobobobobleLL UP. A CIRglibibibibibibiCUS L E g l u b b a g l u b b a g l u b b a G E N D RbleblebbleblebleETURNS – oh, this is useless.'

Armitage tossed his loudhailer to the ground and marched off in a huff, m u t t e r i n g something a b o u t one day cooking a camel casserole with hump sauce, but the damage had already been done.

Much of Ernesto's audience had bought tickets for Armitage's show.

By the time the curtain went up, there was one Big Top's worth of audience, divided more or less equally between the two shows. This was phase one of Armitage's plan. Phase two was more elaborate, and was due to commence during the circus.

Since the defection of Hank, Frank and Jesse to Ernesto's troupe, Armitage had hired some replacements, which meant a change of direction for his circus, and not just by adding the words 'very extreme' to the title, which was a temporary measure.

With only Maurice, Irrrrena and Fingers O'Boyle left from his original show, Armitage had needed new performers, but there were three problems:

1) Armitage demanded a high level of circus

expertise, combined with at least two years of advanced criminal experience, from all his acts.

2) It wasn't possible to advertise for criminals, so he had to hire people he already knew.

3) Everyone who knew Armitage disliked him intensely, and would never want to work for him.

These problems foxed Armitage for a long time, until one day, after a long broody, grumpy sulk, he came up with a single solution to all three.☺

Animals!

Even though Armitage hadn't been impressed by Queenie Bombazine's pathetic, paltry, putrid, pitiful puddle of a circus, he had to concede that the audience had liked the animal stuff: the synchronised otters, the piano tuna, the sea lion thing, all that malarkey had gone down a treat with the punters. Perhaps he could do something a

---

☺ Armitage had most of his best ideas during sulks. He found them very productive. Showering was his other main source of inspiration. He enjoyed showers so much that he found it very hard to sulk during one, but on the rare occasions that he managed a simultaneous sulk/shower, he often came up with a real humdinger.

bit like that. But dry.

So it wasn't even a stolen idea – it was completely original – because he was going to do it out of the water! Armitage wouldn't steal other people's ideas. Oh, no. He was an impresario, a Svengali, a creative visionary, not some mediocre rip-off merchant. He'd steal pretty much anything off anybody, but never an idea. Queenie's work was simply a launch pad, an inspiration, a starting point for Armitage's unique imaginative endeavours.

Or so he claimed.

Plus, if he got the right animals and trained them well enough, perhaps he could teach them to take part in the odd burglary. If they got caught, so what? The police don't lock up animals, even if they're caught in the act of taping explosives to a safe.

It would be the perfect crime. A sort of

mafia zoo.

But that was for the future. For now, he just needed performing animals.

Armitage had been formulating his comeback for a while, and so far he had recruited:

- Six performing monkeys, whose act involved pick-pocketing things from the audience, then returning things to the wrong people, to comic effect. (Yes, they were already in training for future criminal projects.)

- A mathematical pig. Which was a pig who did maths. It's more entertaining than it sounds. (Armitage had his eye on a little creative accountancy in the long term, but hadn't yet figured out how to make this work.)

- A lleaping llama. (Self-explanatory. No criminal outlet yet devised for this one.)

- A canary choir, capable of singing a quite brilliant medley of Eighties hits, including 'Eye of the Tiger' and 'Wake Me Up Before You Go-Go'. Armitage had paid through the nose for these birds, purchasing them direct from the legendary duck breeder Mac McMack, but it seemed worth it. (They'd pan out as top-of-the-range lookouts in the long run.)

Maurice and Irrrrena were unimpressed by this change of direction, until Armitage pointed out that the proceeds of their crimes could now be divided into fewer, larger chunks. As long as the animals were fed, they didn't need to be paid. After that, Maurice and Irrrrena's 'un' evaporated, leaving them impressed.

Fingers loved the idea, especially the monkeys. And the more disobedient and mischievous the monkeys became, the more he loved them. Disobedience and mischief were the two qualities Fingers strove for in his own work, so this was hardly surprising.

In order not to get confused, Fingers named the monkeys Monday, Tuesday, Wednesday, Thursday, Friday and Cuddlecakes. There was an element of favouritism here, but you couldn't help noticing that Cuddlecakes had star quality. His pick-pocketing skills verged on genius. In Cuddlecakes, Fingers had at long last found his soulmate.

Fingers taught him to play chess, and Cuddlecakes soon began to win, even though Fingers cheated, mainly because Cuddlecakes cheated, too, but better.

Even Maurice got over his initial scepticism, and ended up teaching the canary choir to sing the 'Marseillaise'.♪

Irrrrena took a shine to the mathematical pig, who had the unusual name of 3.14159 (or Pi for short, which is, in turn, short for pig). Irrrrena and 3.14159 often whiled away whole afternoons together doing Sudoku. 3.14159 also gave great

---

♪ This is the French national anthem, the lyrics of which are something along the lines of:
France is really cool, Oooh yeah.
Much, much cooler than everywhere else.
With really nice cheese and everything,
Oooh, so cool, so, so cool.

(As opposed to the British national anthem, which goes:
The Queen is really cool, Ooooh, yeah.
Much, much cooler than everyone else,
With sometimes slightly above average cheese and everything.
Oooh, slightly above average)

back massages. Irrrrena had to keep it to herself just how good these massages were, because Maurice was prone to fits of atrocious jealousy.

It isn't necessary to go into all the details of Armitage's show right now. What's important is that roughly halfway through the second half, Armitage, as usual, sneaked out. You can probably guess where he went.

He headed straight for Ernesto Espadrille's box office – and not to buy a ticket. This was the big surprise he had been bragging about, which, to be honest, wasn't really much of a surprise at all.

It didn't take him long to pick the lock.

Nor did it take him long to attach explosives to Ernesto's safe.

But when the safe-cracking device went off, he discovered something unexpected and deeply unpleasant. Not a penny was in there. The safe wasn't empty, however. It was filled with a black,

glutinous, gloopy, fishy and very, very stinky
substance. Squid ink. Two-week-old squid ink.

Take it from me. This stuff honks. It honks

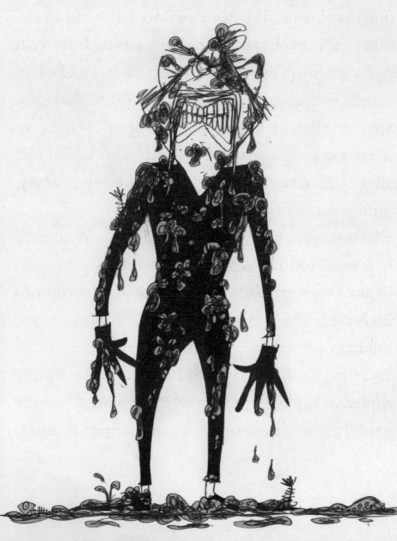

about as much as three hundred geese fighting over one nest. That is pretty honky.

If you are unfortunate enough to blow up a safe filled with this stuff, and you are standing in the same room, you are going to emerge from that room smelling worse than you have smelled in your whole life. Quite probably, you will also be angrier than you have ever been, which in Armitage's case made you quite extraordinarily angry – about as angry as two hundred and ninety-nine homeless geese.

Armitage knew straight away what had happened to him, which isn't to say that he could identify the variety of stinky gloop that had doused his body, but he realised Ernesto had booby-trapped the safe.

Yet again, Armitage had been kippered – or, in this case, squidded. The burglary had not gone to plan. This was more or less as off-plan as a burglary could go.

But little did he know, worse was to come. Because while he'd been away drenching himself in a surprise explosion of rancid cephalopod juice, something truly bizarre had taken place in the Circus Impossible Big Top – something so bizarre it was almost, but not quite, impossible.

TWELVE

Zachary rises and devises more surprises in disguises

WHO WAS BEHIND THIS BIZARRE-TO-the-point-of-impossible event?

Zachary Shank, of course. But to explain his scheme we must rewind to earlier in the day.

Chippy, Zachary, Vince and Frankie had holed up in Zachary's van on Hockney Marshes for most of the afternoon, watching events unfold,[6] trying to figure out how it was that these two rival circuses

---

[6] Events are always unfolding everywhere, all the time. Who it is that folds them up in the first place is a mystery.

had suddenly popped up in the same place at the same time to compete for the same audience. It didn't make any sense.

But Zachary wasn't worried about that. His mind was on one thing and one thing only: diddling his brother.

Zachary knew his window of opportunity would be when Armitage went out stealing. All he had to do was wait, watch and be ready to pounce.

Sure enough, halfway through the second half, the four men watched Armitage tiptoe from the bigger Big Top to his caravan, pop in for a moment, then pop out again dressed in full burglarising gear. He then scurried off in the direction of the Espadrille box office (unaware at this point that an anti-squid scuba-diving outfit would probably have been a wiser choice of clothes).

This was the moment.

'This is it,' said Zachary. 'Action stations, lads.

Let's go. *Danununununununa noo noo nunanuna boof boof digadigadig!*'

'What's *Danununununununa noo noo nunanuna boof boof digadigadig*?' asked Vince.

'It's my action stations theme music. But that's not important right now. Let's go!'

They sprinted towards Armitage's caravan, where Zachary stilled the other three with an outstretched arm. 'Right,' he said. 'Chippy, you stand guard at the Big Top. Not the little Big Top. The big Big Top. Frankie, you stay here. Vince, you come in with me. You're going to do my make-up.'

'Your what?' said Vince, who really wasn't getting any less confused by what on earth was going on.

'You saw that hideously ugly ratty skunk of a man who just sneaked out of this caravan? I need you to make me look like him.'

'But you already look like him,' said Vince, who

might have realised this was an impolite comment if he hadn't been in such an advanced state of bafflement.

'WHAT DID YOU SAY?' barked Zachary.

'Er . . . I mean . . . I don't know much about make-up and I don't know how I'll . . . you know . . . figure out how to make you look so completely different . . . but I'll . . . er—'

'Shut yer mouth and follow me.'

Zachary skipped up the steps, picked the lock on Armitage's caravan and disappeared inside. Vince followed.

Zachary was already stripping off and dressing himself in Armitage's discarded ringmaster's outfit. This proved to be something of a challenge, since the trousers were already as tight as is humanly possible on Armitage, and Zachary's fondness for eel pies had given him a waistline several sizes larger. In the end, Vince had to lift him off the ground and lower him into the trousers, having caked his legs in a kilo or two of talcum powder. Luckily, the seams were triple-stitched or the garment would have exploded like a safe filled with squid ink.⁓&

Fully costumed, Zachary couldn't bend at the knees or waist, and his voice was an octave or two higher than usual, but after an extremely amateurish application of stage make-up, everyone had to admit he was now almost indistinguishable from his hideous twin.

'Look at me,' said Zachary, admiring himself in one of Armitage's four full-length mirrors. "Nuff to make you puke, ain't it?'

'Yes . . . I mean, no . . . I mean . . . no comment,' said Vince, struggling to think of the least insulting response.

'Right,' said Zachary. 'Show time! *Yadadadada shwwwwing yugada shwwwwing chachaaaaa!'*

⁓&One of Armitage's many mottoes was 'Cut every corner you can and skimp on everything. *Except clothes.'*

This time, Vince didn't ask. He'd figured this one out for himself. That was clearly Zachary's show time theme.

'*Yadadadada shwwwwing yugada shwwwwing chachaaaaa!*' sang Zachary and Frankie and Vince as they ran back across Hockney Marshes towards the Circus Impossible Big Top. Well, Frankie and Vince ran; Zachary kind of waddled, due to the non-bending-trouser situation.

THIRTEEN
The invisible hand of Esmeralda Espadrille

*B*UT WHAT ABOUT HANNAH?

Yes, yes, I know.

You left her hanging there in mid-air, swaying and tipping above the hole in her safety net! Moments away from meeting her doooooom!

Oh, come on. Surely you know me better than that. I couldn't let Hannah meet her dooooom. Not here – right in the middle of a book. She's our heroine.

She could still have fallen. I mean, you could have broken her legs or something.

Stop that! I won't have you butting in with your horrible and inappropriate ideas. I will *not* break Hannah's legs – not here, not anywhere, not ever.

What about her nose?

Stop it! I don't know who you are, but it's time for you to go away and interrupt someone else.

Right. Where were we? Ah, yes. Hannah was up on her tightrope, swaying and tipping, her concentration shattered by the noise of the blown-up safe.

Speaking of the safe, you'll be pleased to hear that's how Hannah ended up. No, not blown up. Safe.

She made it back down from her tightrope despite throbbing thighs, knocking knees, shivering shins, clammy calves, anxious ankles, fretful feet and trembling toes. She gave a small and very modest bow, thinking she had entirely messed up her act, but the audience, who had witnessed her tussle with *doooom*, and seen the bravery, skill and concentration required to get her performance back on track, were so relieved and impressed that they all rose to their feet and gave an ear-splitting standing ovation. Only one person in the entire audience didn't join in. Wanda. Because she had fainted. Again.

Hannah hurried from the stage, anxious that Ernesto might tell her off, or sack her, or even just be disappointed in her for getting things wrong, but in the two seconds between her exit and his entrance, he looked deep into her eyes and said, with absolute sincerity, 'I'm so proud of you! You were brilliant! That was true circus.'

'Thank you,' said Hannah, her eyes filling with tears. This was the best compliment anyone had ever paid her.

'Now I need you to do something,' he continued. 'Armitage is trying to rob us. That bang was him blowing up my safe. He hasn't got anything yet, because it was booby-trapped, but you never know what he'll do next. Find him and stop him. I can't help. I'm on.' And with that, he was off.

Ernesto cartwheeled away into the ring (which isn't an easy thing to do when you're riding a unicycle) leaving Hannah in an addled, muddled and befuddled state of mind as she watched him from the wings. She couldn't look for Armitage just yet. Her heart was still thrumming, not just with fear, but also with an exquisite and uplifting sensation she had never felt before. Hannah realised she had at last experienced the true essence of circus, and it was like silken gloves massaging her very soul.

But there was something else. Something more than that. Something so powerful it held her transfixed. In those last minutes, up on that tightrope, facing real danger, Hannah had come closer to her mother – her real mother – than ever before. It was as if she had felt her physical presence for the first time.

She still wasn't quite sure what had stopped her falling, what had stilled her panicking mind and toppling body, but at the key moment she had felt the distinct sensation of two gentle, reassuring hands placing themselves calmly on her shoulders. She hadn't been able to turn and look, but she was sure she recognised the touch. Her mother, the mother she had never even met, was right there with her, guiding her to safety.

'Hannah? Are you OK?' Billy asked. Her eyes were wide and far, far away. She hadn't even heard him approach.

'I'm fine,' she said. 'More than fine. I've never felt better. Aren't you supposed to be on stage?'

'I should be, but this is an emergency. Dad's going solo. We've got work to do. Let's go.'

'I . . . I felt her,' said Hannah.

'Who?'

'Our mother.'

'When?'

'On the tightrope. She was there. She saved me.'

'I know.'

'You know?'

'I felt it, too. I didn't see her, but I sensed her up there, with you. I closed my eyes and wished for her help.'

'You did?'

'I did. She isn't gone. She's always here. In this Big Top. She's always watching. But . . .'

'But what?'

'But we have to go. Now. Armitage is getting away.'

And off they went, in pursuit, yet again, of that cranky, crazed, creepy, cretinous, crooked, crafty criminal, Armitage Shank.

FOURTEEN

Zachary does Armitage while Armitage does Ernesto while Ernesto does some juggling

AT THE SAME MOMENT THAT HANNAH and Billy set off in search of Armitage, and Armitage staggered inkily and stinkily out of Ernesto's box office, Zachary stepped onto his twin brother's stage, in disguise.

He tried to prance. He knew that prancing was important in the circus game, but unfortunately it isn't possible to prance without bending at the knees. He tried a couple of prancey strides, but

---

If you don't believe me, sellotape a ruler firmly to each leg and attempt a prance. You won't manage it. And you'll probably break your rulers.

soon realised that he was goose-stepping, which felt very wrong, so he settled for the closest he could get to a standard walk, given the trouser situation.

Zachary had never been on stage before. He'd never had so many people stare at him with such happy faces, waiting for him to entertain them. It felt like the biggest hug of his life. The feeling was just overwhelmingly lovely, so much so that he momentarily forgot he actually had to do something other than just stand there basking in the circussy glow.

No sooner did he remember that he needed to put on an act, than he also remembered that he didn't have an act to put on. But that wasn't the point. He wasn't there to entertain. He was there to sabotage. He was there, in the guise of his despicable lorry-loving brother, to make the audience hate him so much that they asked for

their money back, thereby creating the biggest mass-robbery of Armitage that was humanly possible, which would take all his takings for the evening, and at the same time swamp him with such an angry mob that Zachary would be able to take anything that the takings-takers weren't taking for themselves. If things went really well, Zachary would be able to steal the Big Top itself.

That was the plan. Entertainment had nothing to do with his purpose on stage. He was there to make the audience hate him (or at least, to make them hate the person they thought he was).

But when that spotlight hit him, something curious happened. A distinct flush appeared on Zachary's face. A glow seemed to rise to his cheeks, giving him an appearance of serenity and happiness that Chippy, Vince and Frankie had never seen before. Serene happiness was not Zachary's standard demeanour.

Zachary had been hit by a feeling not dissimilar to the one that had overwhelmed Hannah after finishing her act. Some indefinable, impalpable, inexplicable circus magic had sprinkled itself over him and seemingly rewired his brain. To put it another way, Zachary was stage-struck.

This was a problem since, according to his original plan, he was there purely to annoy the audience so much that they demanded a refund.

But given the stage-struck situation, which had now overtaken the trouser situation as Zachary's main concern, he decided to make a slight modification to his original scheme. He didn't need to start irritating the audience straight away. What was the rush? This might be the only opportunity he'd ever get to perform in a Big Top. It would be a shame to pass it up without at least having a go at circussing.

The problem was, he didn't know how to do

anything except steal, swindle and intimidate, none of which are very circussy activities.

Then he remembered something. Like his brother, Zachary loved to shower, and in the shower he always sang. It had often struck Zachary, while singing in the shower, that his voice was at least as good, if not better, than the warbling, whiny weirdoes whose songs filled the radio airwaves.

I could do that, he'd often thought to himself.

And now he could. He had an audience. He had a microphone. It was time to treat the world to a stage debut of his vocal skills.

'LADIES and gentlemen, BOYS and girls, and anyone else who doesn't fall into the above-mentioned categories, WELCOME to the Circus Impossible Extreme Something Wassitcalled Thingummy CIRCUS!! Yes! Here I am, Zach— . . . er, I mean Armitage Shank . . . ringmaster extraordinaire . . . here to thrill and entertain you with my . . . er . . . circus. Which you've already seen some of. Obviously. And I hope you liked it! Of course you did! Hooray!'

Zachary took a few goose-stepping prance-attempts, stopped himself, and cracked Armitage's whip. Or tried to. He tried four times, but a whip in the hands of a non-expert whipcracker isn't much more than an oversized shoelace, which, flapped silently in the air, provides very little entertainment value.

'Blast,' he spat, chucking the whip to the ground. 'Anyway . . . what was I saying? Yes! WELCOME! And that kind of stuff! And it is my pleasure as your ringmaster extraordinaire, ARMITAGE Shank, to treat you . . . before our next wonderful act . . . to a song.'

Zachary raised his arms and attempted a cartwheel. It didn't go well.

'Blast,' he muttered, dusting himself down. 'This sawdust is much too slippery. Anyway. What was I saying? I think I've got a splinter. Er . . . yes! A song! Written by me as a tribute to my hero, Mr Bung Crosby, probably the greatest crooner of the century. Not this century. The last one. Crooners these days are a bunch of amateurs, if you ask me. Anyway, here goes. You'll just have to imagine the band because I don't have one. It's called 'Lovey, lovey, love love'. It's a love song.'

Zachary began to sing. If he thought he was replacing his plan to annoy the audience with an alternative, he was very much mistaken, because his singing wasn't well received. Not at all.

I love youuu,

Yes I doooo.

You love me toooo.

You're very nice.

And so am I!

That's probably why we love each other.
Ooooh!
Lovey, lovey, love love.

His voice was approximately sixty-seven thousand times less good than Zachary thought it was. The audience began to boo.

Let's hold hands, don't fret.
Let's go for a walk in the sunset
Near to where we first met.
You have lovely hands.
And feet.
But especially hands.
And so do I.
But that's not why we love each other.
Ooooh!
Lovely, lovey, love love.

The boos turned into jeers, then shouts. Some people wept in despair. Others begged for mercy.

'You're rubbish!'

'Get off!'

'Where's the next act?'

'PLEASE STOP SINGING!'

'WE WANT OUR MONEY BACK!'

At the sound of the word 'money', Zachary snapped out of his fantasy of vocal stardom and realised that his performance was not getting the reception he had anticipated. In fact, it was getting the reception he had planned to get for being deliberately bad, but as a response to his attempt to be deliberately good.

The blush of pleasure left Zachary's cheeks. He went white. Another blush rose, this one of embarrassment (in the left cheek) and rage (in the right cheek).

All these years he had dreamed that he was an

undiscovered crooning genius, destined to wow the world with his unique and original songbook. But now, in a sudden and brutal way, he learned that he'd overestimated his appeal. He was not, after all, a great singer. He was not even a good singer. He was rubbish. Nobody liked his song. Nobody liked his singing. Nobody liked him.

For a moment, Zachary thought he might be about to cry. Then a surge of pure white-hot jealousy for his brother sparkled through his veins. Why was it that Armitage knew how to do this and not him? How was it that his hideous fink of a sibling knew how to go on a stage and make strangers like him, when within a matter of seconds Zachary had made an entire audience loathe him? It wasn't fair. Why did people like Armitage more? Why? Why?

As the wave of shouts from the crowd grew ever louder, Zachary suddenly remembered where he was and what he was supposed to be doing. He was in the middle of a plan to diddle his brother. He wanted the audience to hate him, and he'd achieved that in record time. Yes, he was good at what he did. He was a criminal, and a skilful one, unlike his useless brother, who could be relied on to always mess up his burglarising. Zachary had nothing to be ashamed of. Circussing was a stupid waste of time, anyway. So what if Armitage knew how to prance around on stage entertaining people? Pah! That was no job for a fully grown man! What a waste of time!

'Right, you horrible, useless bunch of grinning morons,' yelled Zachary. 'You don't like my singing? So what! I don't care! I don't like you, either! And if you think coming into this stupid tent and watching stupid people do stupid things is sensible, then you're . . . er . . . stupid. So there.'

A stunned silence filled the Big Top, followed by

more than a hundred splutters of outrage, followed by a tsunami of booing.

'If you don't like it, lump it,'❓he shouted. 'And if you can't lump it, then come and find me in my caravan. It's the big shiny silver one just outside the Big Top. I'm going there right now to count the money I made from selling tickets to you idiots. If you shout enough and beat the door down I might consider giving you a refund, but you'll have to get really angry because the truth is **CIRCUSES ARE RUBBISH, INCLUDING THIS ONE, AND PEOPLE WHO GO TO THEM ARE ALL DUNCES WHO DESERVE TO BE RIPPED OFF! AND I *AM* A GOOD SINGER – YOU JUST DON'T KNOW ANYTHING ABOUT MUSIC. I'M THE NEXT BUNG CROSBY! MARK MY WORDS!'**

More silence. Proper silence this time, since everyone in the audience was now too shocked to even boo.

❓ This doesn't mean anything, but everyone understood what he meant. Sometimes complete nonsense is just as clear as perfect clarity. At other times, nonsense is just nonsense. This footnote is roughly halfway between sensible nonsense and nonsense nonsense. Halfway nonsense of this kind is sometimes known as pointless nonsense, which is an accurate name for it, and explains why we need to stop wasting our time down here and go back up the page in search of some sensible nonsense.

'THIS CIRCUS IS OVER!' Zachary continued. 'GO HOME!'

Then he sprinted off the stage, which finally resolved the trouser situation. There was a loud ripping noise as he fled, and the audience found themselves staring aghast at a stage containing nothing but a trouser-shaped shred of black cloth.

FIFTEEN

Never trust a monkey

MAURICE, IRRRRENA AND FINGERS O'Boyle watched this spectacle from the wings, increasingly convinced that Armitage had gone insane.

None of them had thought he was particularly sane in the first place, but even for Armitage this was bizarre.

Trouserless, sprinting Zachary barged straight into them, thinking he'd be able to knock Maurice out of the way. He didn't realise that, though

Maurice was small, his muscles had the consistency of reinforced concrete, and Zachary simply bounced off him, falling flat on his back.

'What was that?' said Fingers. 'What were you doing out there?'

'You're fired!' Zachary snapped, hauling himself back to his feet. 'All of you. As of now. HahahaHA.' (He wasn't nearly as good at cackling as his brother.) 'And I'm doing you a favour! Because all of this stupid circus rubbish is just . . . a load of . . . stupid rubbish. Ha! Those morons wouldn't know a good song if it drove through their ears and parked in their brain.'

Zachary stormed away, leaving the three fired performers standing there in the wings, listening to a deluge of booing, jeering and cat-calling▪from the auditorium.

'What do we do now?' said Fingers.

'I don't know,' said Maurice.

▪ Cat-calling, in this context, means loud and angry whistling, not going down on your knees and saying, 'Here puss-puss, time for kitty din-dins,' which is also cat-calling, but would be a strange response to unprovoked insults from a crooning half-naked ringmaster.

'What are you talking about?' snapped Irrrrena. 'Of course you know. What are you? Civilians?'

Fingers and Maurice stared at her, confused.

'No!' continued Irrrrena. 'You're circussers. And, fired or not fired, you go out there, in the name of circus, and save the show. Now. NOW!'

Fingers knew she was right.

He had no idea how he'd do it, but he knew it was a matter of honour that he at least try. Fingers didn't usually have much time for the concept of honour. He was a thief, after all. But this was circus honour, which is different. Circus honour is about never disappointing your audience: it is a sacred code stating that whatever happens, come what may, the show must go on.

Fingers shuffled into the ring, where he was greeted not by the usual cheers and smiles, but by a barrage of angry noise.

'Thank you very much, there, to our new clown

. . . Zongo, who was trying out some experimental material. So – sorry about that. But now, back to the show! I'm Fingers O'Boyle, and I'd like you to welcome onto the stage my troupe of thieving monkeys!'

At this point in the performance, the audience usually did what was asked, and welcomed on stage the thieving monkeys. This time, the greeting was different.

'WE'VE HAD ENOUGH THIEVING ALREADY!'

'WE WANT OUR MONEY BACK!'

'THIS IS THE WORST CIRCUS I'VE EVER SEEN!'

'Ladies and gentlemen, please be patient. And here they are: Monday, Tuesday, Wednesday, Thursday, Friday and Cuddlecakes!'

The monkeys came on stage, took one look at the angry audience, and ran off again.

'Monday! Tuesday! Come back!' begged Fingers. 'Cuddlecakes! Don't leave! Please!'

'GET OFF!'

'RUBBISH!'

'YOU'RE EVEN WORSE THAN THE LAST ACT!'

'MY DAUGHTER'S BEEN LOOKING FORWARD TO THIS FOR MONTHS, NOW SHE'S IN TEARS! YOU SHOULD BE ASHAMED OF YOURSELF.'

'WHAT A RIP-OFF!'

Fingers was a man blessed with great panache and confidence, but we all have our limits. Every drop of self-assurance drained out him, and the only thing he wanted now was to save himself further humiliation and get off that stage.

He ran out of the ring so fast that he bumped straight into Maurice, which of course bounced him right back into the ring, flat on his bum. This got a small laugh from the audience, but not the kind of laugh a performer wants.

He got back to his feet and scurried away.

'I think the show's over,' Maurice said to Irrrrena, his face white with dread.

'One last try,' she said. 'My mother taught me never to give up. And how to make lemon drizzle cake. That was about it. Now let's go.'

Irrrrena pushed Maurice into the ring, then pranced out confidently, somersaulting, cartwheeling and back-flipping.

Maurice's circus instincts kicked in, and his king-of-all-prances led him to centre stage, where he plucked a hand-springing Irrrrena from mid-air and held her standing upright in one raised palm. His muscles bulged and quivered, and the audience quietened down a little.

'AT LEAST YOU CAN DO SOMETHING.'

'YOU'RE GOOD, BUT WE STILL WANT OUR

MONEY BACK!'

'HOW DID HE GET SO SHINY?'

By the time the canary choir was on stage singing the 'Marseillaise', the audience had stopped heckling.

But they still wanted a refund.

SIXTEEN

The chapter so short it doesn't deserve a title

AND WHERE WERE HANNAH AND BILLY all this time? Still hunting for Armitage?

Why am I asking you? If I don't know, how are you supposed to know?

What's happened? We need an author, here, who has some idea of what's going on. Get a grip!

Right. Yes – Hannah and Billy were still on the hunt for their thieving nemesis, but not very effectively, since they had no idea where he was.

'Where are we going?' gasped Hannah, who was still out of breath from her tightrope act (and from almost falling to her *doooom* (and from her moment of mystical communion with her trapeze-artist birth mother (you're not really allowed to do this with brackets but I don't care (I like brackets (sometimes))))).

'To stop Armitage.'

'Stop him doing what?'

'Stealing.'

'Stealing what?'

'Anything.'

'But where is he?'

'I don't know.'

'So why are we running?'

'I don't know,' said Billy, without slowing down.

'Shall we stop?'

'Why?'

'Because we don't know where we're going.'

'Then we should keep running, because we'll be able to rule out all the wrong places to look quicker than if we walk.'

'WAIT!' said Hannah, grabbing Billy's arm. 'Listen.'

Billy listened.

They heard a noise that sounded like a cross between a song and a circular saw cutting through metal, followed by the unmistakable sound of an audience booing.

'What is that?' said Billy.

'I think it's somebody doing some metalwork.'

'I reminds me of a record Armitage used to play by a guy called Bung Crosby. I think it might be somebody trying to sing one of his songs. It sounds a bit like Armitage, but even worse.'

'I've thought of a plan!' said Hannah. 'Even if we can't find Armitage, we can stop him getting away.'

'How?'

'The enormous lorry! We can siphon off the petrol.'

'That's genius,' said Billy.

'Except that I don't know how to do it.'

'I do. It's easy. Armitage taught me when I was about three. He always said that after walking and talking, siphoning petrol is one of life's most important skills.'

'Great! Let's do it,' said Hannah, turning and running in the direction of the enormous lorry.

Wanda, meanwhile, having come round from her last faint just in time to see Hannah descend safely to the ground, was finally enjoying the circus. Watching Ernesto, the man her sister had married, leap, bound, spring, float and fly around the stage, dressed in an admirably figure-hugging outfit, Wanda appreciated, for the first time, the appeal of this kind of entertainment. She also understood, at long last, why her sister had wanted to run away from a safe and healthy house to the risky and dangerous environment of the circus. Because this man was, quite simply, magnificent.

Wanda always thought her sister had been crazy to run away. Now she thought maybe she'd been crazy to stay at home. Wendy's life may have been short, but she'd really lived. Wanda's life had been long, but . . . well . . . predictable.

The strange mixture of enjoyment, regret, wonder, grief, fondness, jealousy, admiration, relief and yearning coursing through Wanda's heart left her so confused that, by the end of Ernesto's act, she couldn't even tell if she was happy or sad. The truth is, she was both at once.

SEVENTEEN
It can be useful to smell of rotten fish

WE HAVEN'T SEEN ARMITAGE FOR A while, have we? Can you guess what kind of mood he was in? Of course you can: stinky. And can you remember how he was smelling? Of course you can: stinky. And can you think of a word that rhymes with pinkie? Of course you c—

STOP THAT NONSENSE! THERE'S A STORY GOING ON HERE!

OK. Where were we?

Armitage had just exploded a booby-trapped safe and was covered in rotten squid ink, which, unbeknownst🕮to him, had been sent especially for this purpose straight from Queenie Bombazine's new aquarium. He was not a happy ringmaster. But suddenly – KERCHING! – a dastardly glint glinted glintily out from the two devious, criminal eyes which were the only un-inked parts of his dark, squiddy face.

Armitage had formulated a plan. This hideous smell crawling up his nostrils reminded him of something.

It reminded him of taramasalata.

Which reminded him of Narcissus.

Which gave him an idea.

Armitage stopped stomping (which is how he walked when he was in a sulk) and began to tiptoe (which is how he walked when he was burglarising).

🕮 'Unbeknownst' is a book word. Nobody ever says it in real life. Other examples are moreover, nevertheless and jumbohubbanoops. (Though one of those words has only ever appeared in one book.)

He tiptoed in the direction of a certain cage, containing a certain camel, who was at that moment wondering why he hadn't been led on stage for the Circus Extreme finale. But when Narcissus' nostrils began to pick up the exquisite scent of rotten squid ink, he immediately stopped thinking about the strangeness of his omission from the performance. Every one of his brain cells diverted to his favourite topic: seafood.

Narcissus was extremely surprised by what then came into view. Not a large platter of taramasalata. Not even a small platter of taramasalata or any other marine delicacy, but a man covered in squid juice. A man he recognised as his former owner. A man he did not like one little bit.

Until now.

Now Narcissus liked the look of Armitage very much indeed. In fact, he was immediately overwhelmed by the desire to lick him all over. He had never before wanted to lick any human as much as he now wanted to lick this man.

Armitage rapidly picked the lock on Narcissus' cage. Narcissus then hurried out and began to lick. Oh, boy, was this squid ink gorgeous. Ripe, mature, fruity, with subtle woody notes of citrus and bergamot and a quite exquisite honk of off fish. Deeeeeelicious.

Armitage did not enjoy the experience quite so much. As a rule, he tried to avoid camel goo and now he was getting caked in the stuff, which is like smearing yourself in rancid lard. It was also the most ticklish experience of his entire life and Armitage, you won't be surprised to hear, did not like being tickled.

But it was worth it. Because this was all part of his plan.

'Come on, boy,' said Armitage. 'Follow me. Come on.'

Narcissus didn't hear a word Armitage said, because his entire brain was flooded with the message, 'SQUID! SQUID! SQUID! SQUID! SQUID! SQUID! SQUID!'

But that doesn't mean he failed to follow, because wherever Armitage and his gourmet topping went, Narcissus was going, too.

Where was Armitage going?

To his enormous lorry, of course.

Why?

Kidnap!

Yes, this was Armitage's new plan. He was going to lure Narcissus into his enormous lorry and kidnap him. Camelnap him. For a ransom.

Revenge! And theft! And money! Three of Armitage's favourite things, all wrapped up in a parcel of heavenly deviousness!

Getting covered from head to toe in camel goo wasn't exactly fun, but with three pros and only one con, this counted as a top-notch plan – a plan he felt sure couldn't possibly fail.

When Armitage got to his enormous lorry, for a moment he thought he glimpsed something suspicious. Two children running away from somewhere near the fuel tank, holding something that looked like a length of rubber tubing. But since Narcissus was at that moment licking Armitage's face, he couldn't be quite sure, because mostly he just saw a rubbery, inky camel tongue.

During a momentary gap between laps, Armitage thought he saw another strange thing. He thought he glimpsed four men climbing into

the cabin of his lorry, but that seemed unlikely. One of them looked as if he was wearing a ringmaster's jacket and no trousers. He also looked strangely familiar. There was something he recognised about that long moustache and those hideous teeth.

But only a criminal mastermind would know how to pick the enormous locks on the enormous doors of his enormous lorry, and only a ringmaster would walk around in a ringmaster's jacket, and since Armitage was right there, what were the chances that another ringmaster-cum-criminal-mastermind with a long moustache and hideous

teeth would be at the same spot at the same time? Pretty much zero.

Armitage concluded that the goo fumes must be going to his head. He was clearly hallucinating.

Just as Armitage was coaxing Narcissus through the back doors of the lorry by offering him a particularly squiddy armpit, the vehicle jerked into motion.

Armitage fell out.

Narcissus fell out.

On top of Armitage.

You don't need to have personal experience of a camel landing on top of you to be able to guess what this felt like.

Here is a clue: sore. Very sore. Certainly sore enough to dispel the idea that anything you are experiencing might be a hallucination.

Armitage looked up at Narcissus, howled in pain, and revised his theory that another ringmaster-cum-criminal-mastermind with a long moustache and hideous teeth couldn't be at the same spot at the same time.

It was clear that he really had seen the person he thought he might have seen. And thinking back, he realised he recognised that long moustache and those hideous teeth and that pair of hairy knees. He knew who it was!

Armitage had no idea why this person was dressed as a trouserless ringmaster, but he knew for certain who he'd seen climbing into his lorry.

It was his brother!

Zachary!

His long-lost twin!

His sibling and deadly rival!

Zachary was BACK!

And he had stolen the enormous lorry!

Which he'd been trying to do for Armitage's WHOLE LIFE!

And now he'd done it!

Not a tiny enormous lorry, but the enormous enormous lorry!

Lying there, squashed into Hockney Marshes by the full weight of a dromedary, smeared in a cocktail of camel goo and rancid squid ink, having just committed a failed burglary and a failed camelnap, after which his most hated enemy had stolen his most beloved vehicle, Armitage admitted to himself that his plan not gone to plan. Neither of his plans had gone to plan. Both of them, in fact, had been quite disastrous.

The only positive thought in Armitage's head was that at least the day couldn't get any worse.

'Pfffffffffffffffffffffp,' said Narcissus, and not with his mouth, producing an odour that proved Armitage's last idea very wrong indeed.

EIGHTEEN

Armitage and Narcissus get into an unusual argument

NO SOONER HAD HANNAH AND BILLY done their siphoning than the enormous lorry roared off. Hannah stared in disbelief. Had Armitage got into the lorry without them noticing? And how had he driven away without any fuel?

'I thought we siphoned off the petrol!'

'There's probably a little bit left in the engine,' said Billy. 'He won't get far.'

'Should we follow him?'

'Maybe we should. Hang on. What's that?'

Billy pointed to a camel-shaped lump that was now visible just behind where the enormous lorry had been parked.

The camel-shaped lump stood up. It was a camel. It was Narcissus.

A human-shaped lump lay groaning on the ground.

Narcissus began to lick the human-shaped lump.

The human-shaped lump stood up. It was Armitage.

'GET OFF!' yelled Armitage. 'GET OFF ME, YOU HORRIBLE CAMEL. I'VE HAD ENOUGH. STOP LICKING ME.'

Narcissus carried on licking Armitage.

'GET OFF, GET OFF, GET OFF!'

Armitage walked away. Narcissus followed, still

licking.

Armitage broke into a run. Narcissus broke into a run. Still licking.

Armitage began to sprint in circles, shouting, 'LEAVE ME ALONE! GO AWAY! STOP IT STOP IT STOP IT!'

Narcissus began to sprint in circles, still licking.

'What's going on?' said Hannah.

'I have no idea.'

'If that's Armitage, who was driving the enormous lorry?'

'I have no idea.'

'Why is Narcissus chasing him?'

'No idea.'

'And licking him.'

'No idea.'

'Is that a sign of affection?'

'No, it's a sign of eating.'

'We should call the police. This is the best chance they'll ever get to catch Armitage. He's just blown up a safe, he's got no getaway lorry, and he's distracted by a rampaging camel.'

'You're right. Let's do it.'

'I think he's finally going to be caught,' said Hannah. 'This is the moment we've been waiting for.'

NINETEEN

Zachary goes to plan B

AS THE ENORMOUS LORRY ROARED away, Zachary glimpsed something strange in the rear-view mirror. He saw his brother running round in circles, being chased by a camel who seemed to have mistaken him for a walking lollipop.

Zachary had hoped that Armitage would return to his caravan after the safe-cracking excursion, where he would be mobbed by angry audience members demanding their money back, and hopefully robbing him of all his robbings. This plan clearly hadn't worked, since Armitage was at that moment nowhere near his caravan, and doing something very different from being attacked by a disgruntled audience. Being attacked by a disgruntled camel was probably equally unpleasant, but this was a long way from Zachary's original scheme.

Then an idea struck him – a plan B – a way to make sure Armitage didn't get away with the contents of that safe.

He took out his phone and dialled the number of Ewan Hoozarmy, the retired boxer who worked for Zachary as an occasional bodyguard, enforcer and tough guy.

'Ewan!' he said. 'I got a job for you. Put on a fake police uniform and head for Hockney Marshes. You'll see two Big Tops. Near there is a bloke who looks exactly like me, but isn't me. Arrest him, put him in the van and bring him to my HQ. Got it?'

'OK. Will do, boss,' said Ewan. 'No! Wait!'

'What is it?'

'What does HQ stand for again? Wait! I know! Hooting Queens! No, Hazelnut Quisling! No, Hamburger Quango! No, Humpback Quilter!'

'Headquarters.'

'That's one word. That should just be 'H'.'

'You're getting side-tracked. Have you got the job clear? Can you do it?'

'Yes, boss. Dress as a policeman. Arrest a man who looks like you. Take him to your hindquarters.'

'Headquarters.'

'Headquarters. Got it. I'll be right there as soon as I've finished washing up these spoons.'

'Did you say spoons?'

'I did. I'm washing them up.'

'Interesting. Now hurry. There's no time to waste.'

Zachary hung up, pleased with his plan, but not entirely confident in the skills of Ewan Hoozarmy. He was a vague man at the best of times, and seemed to be in rather an unfocused frame of mind. Too many blows to the head can do that to you. Not that Ewan had ever been the sharpest knife in the cutlery drawer.

But Zachary had given him the job now. He'd just have to hole up at HQ and hope for the best.

'Chugga chugga shplukka tsshhhhhh pfk!' said the enormous lorry, emphasising this statement by jerking to a stop. They hadn't even reached the edge of Hockney Marshes.

'What's going on?' demanded Zachary.

'Empty, boss,' said Vince, tapping the fuel gauge. 'No petrol.'

'How can there be no petrol?'

'Maybe he used it up,' said Chippy.

'Of course he used it up! It was a rhetorical

question, you idiot. What are we going to do now?'

Silence.

After a while, Chippy said, 'Was that a rhetorical question, too?'

'No, you idiot. It was a question question. What are we going to do? DON'T ANSWER! I need to think. I need a plan C.'

TWENTY

999!

HANNAH CALLED THE POLICE. SHE TOLD them that the runaway criminal, ringmaster of the notorious Impossible Circus, Armitage Shank, was on the loose at Hockney Marshes, having just committed the latest attempted robbery in a long career of burglarising. She told them that Armitage had escaped punishment time and again, and this was a perfect opportunity to finally catch him and bring him to justice. She told them exactly where he was, but left out the fact that he was being chased by a hungry camel, since she thought that might sound implausible. She finished by giving them a precise description of his lank moustache and hideous teeth, so they couldn't fail to recognise him.

Did they listen?

Did they?

We're about to find out.

'Look!' said Billy. 'The enormous lorry's stopped!'

Although Hannah and Billy had no idea who was in the enormous lorry or where it was heading, they knew that if Armitage survived Narcissus' attentions, that was where he would go, to reclaim his beloved vehicle. So that was where Hannah and Billy had to go, too. Until the police arrived, it was up to them to monitor Armitage's whereabouts. They couldn't let him get away. Not with arrest so close.

Without having to say another word, they both

set off at a sprint, dashing across Hockney Marshes towards the stranded enormous lorry.⊛

⊛ Don't tell Chapter 15 that Chapter 19 got a title, even though 19 is shorter than the chapter that supposedly didn't get a title because it was too short. 15 would get jealous, and might go off in a sulk, which would leave a confusing hole in the plot. If Chapter 15 asks about Chapter 19, distract it by offering it a biscuit.

TWENTY-ONE

I'm not a man who looks like me!
I am me!

EWAN HOOZARMY ARRIVED AT HOCKNEY Marshes, dressed in his fake policeman's outfit, seventeen and a half jiffies after Zachary's call. That's pretty quick.

He knew he wasn't very good at remembering things, so he had spent every single one of those jiffies muttering to himself, 'Find man who looks like Zachary, arrest him, take him to HQ, find man who looks like Zachary, arrest him, take him to HQ

. . .' over and over again.

The first thing he saw on the marshes was a crowd of angry people shouting at a silver caravan.

That caravan must have really annoyed those people, he thought, but he overrode his natural curiosity on the subject of the irritating caravan, and set about his task of looking for the Zachary lookalike.

Ewan walked between the two Big Tops, among the two audiences who were streaming out into the evening air – half of them looking happy, the other half not. He scanned every face, looking for lank moustaches and hideous teeth, but saw nobody with even the faintest resemblance to his boss.

Then he tripped over something and fell flat into the mud.

A body.

Not a dead body. Just a man, lying down,

exhausted, gasping for breath, smeared all over with something sticky and grey. Next to him was a snoozing, contented, full-looking camel.

Ewan looked again at the man.

He had a moustache. A lank one.

'Are you OK?' asked Ewan.

'No!' snapped the man. 'I am not OK. I am as not OK as it is humanly possible to be.'

As he spoke, Ewan noticed something else. His teeth. They were hideous.

'YOU'RE HIM!' he shouted. 'You're the man who looks like Zachary! Right. What next? Er . . . you're under arrest. I'm arresting you.'

'For what?'

'Er . . . he didn't say.'

'Who didn't say?'

'Er . . . loitering. I'm arresting you for loitering. Come with me.'

Armitage stood up and stared at Ewan. Surely

his day couldn't be getting even worse. There weren't many things more unpleasant than being doused with exploding squid, then squashed, licked, chased, robbed and stink-bombed by a dreadful collaboration of enemies, siblings and dromedaries, but being arrested was one of them. Being arrested was the worst thing of all.

On the other hand, despite the uniform, this person didn't look like a policeman. He didn't talk like a policeman, either. Armitage, who knew a thing or two about disguises, gave Ewan a long, intense stare.

'Who are you?' he demanded.

'Ewan . . . er . . . I mean, a policeman.'

'A policeman?'

'Yes.'

'What's your name?'

'Er . . . Inspector.'

'Inspector what?'

'Inspector Spector.'

'Inspector Spector?'

'Yes. Inspector Hector Spector, of Scotland Yard. And I've been sent on an undercover patrol to arrest loiterers. There's been a spate of it recently. You're the first one I've found, so I'm arresting you.'

'If it's an undercover operation, why are you in uniform?'

'It's a double bluff. Come with me.'

There were many obvious holes in Ewan's story, but since he was roughly twice Armitage's size, none of these holes was of much importance. Ewan simply picked Armitage up and carried him to Zachary's waiting van.

The moment Armitage saw the van, he understood what had happened. On the side of the van were the words, **'ZACHARY SHANK ENTERPRISES: DUCKING/DIVING, IMPORT/**

EXPORT, BARGAIN DESIGNERWEAR, DVDs, PERFUME. BESPOKE LOAN SERVICES ALSO AVAILABLE.' This told Armitage everything he needed to know, not because he wanted to buy some DVDs or perfume, but because he now knew for sure this policeman wasn't a policeman at all. He was one of Zachary's henchmen. His brother clearly didn't just want the enormous lorry. He was after Armitage himself.

Even gripped in the arms of an ex-boxer-cum-fake-policeman, Armitage was still capable of working out a plan to get himself out of a tricky spot. In fact, the trickier the spot, the quicker he thought, and this was, without doubt, a tricky one.

Sure enough, an idea bojangled and bazizzed into his brain right on cue.

'Put me down, you bleedin' oaf, or you're fired!' he said, in his Zachariest voice. 'Ain't you even got 'nuff brains to follow simple instructions? What did I tell you to do?'

Ewan was thrown by the Zachariness of the voice, and began to wonder who this eerily Zachary-like person might be. 'You told me to arrest a man who looks like you, and that's you.'

'I'm not a man who looks like me! I am me!'

'You're you?!'

'Yes! It's me. Zachary!' said Armitage. 'Just after I spoke to you I got drenched with exploding squid and attacked by a hungry camel, which is why I'm not looking proper, but I'm still me. The man who looks like me isn't me – he's him, over there, in that lorry.'

Armitage pointed at the enormous lorry, which was still on the edge of Hockney Marshes. With a start, he realised that the lorry had been in the same spot for a while. Zachary's getaway had stalled.

This was Armitage's chance.

'If you want to keep your job, give me the keys to that van, right now.'

'Er . . . are you sure you're you?'

'Of course I'm me! Look at me! Who else could I be? The me who looks like me looks much less like me than this – because if he looked like this he'd be me! Obviously!'

'Er . . .'

'Just give me the keys.'

'I'll drive,' said Ewan. 'Just in case you're not you. Because if you aren't, how will I explain to the you that is you that I gave away your van to a you who isn't you.'

'I have no idea what you're talking about. Just get in. And follow that enormous lorry.'

TWENTY-TWO

The after-show showdown shows up

YES, IT'S TIME FOR THE CAR CHASE scene.

Except that one of the cars is a lorry.

And it has run out of petrol.

And the other one's a van.

OK, so it's not a very good car chase. It's just a drive, really. Slightly below the speed limit. But anyway, let's not dwell on that. The point is, Armitage, in Zachary's van, soon caught up with

Zachary, in Armitage's lorry.

Armitage leaped out.

Zachary leaped out.

They stared at one another.

Ewan leaped out and stared at both of them.

'Hang on a second,' Ewan said to Armitage. 'You're not you! That's you!'

Armitage and Zachary ignored him. After all these years, the two lank-moustached, hideous-toothed twins were reunited.

They eyed one another, nose to nose, in ominous silence.

For a moment, both of them thought exactly the same thought, namely: I hope my breath doesn't smell like that.

Then Armitage yelled, **'YOU STOLE MY LORRY!'**

'Oh, not that again,' said Zachary. 'When are you going to grow up?'

'When are you going to stop stealing my lorries?'

'When are you going to stop whingeing?'

Chippy, Frankie and Vince were watching this argument in a state of extreme confusion.

'There's two of them,' said Chippy.

'And they hate each other,' added Frankie.

'**ALL MY LIFE YOU'VE BEEN STEALING MY LORRIES! WHAT IS IT WITH YOU AND LORRIES? WHY CAN'T YOU JUST LET ME HAVE A LORRY?**' boomed Armitage.

'**WHY DO YOU HAVE TO SHOW OFF ALL THE TIME?**' boomed Zachary back.

'This is a classic case of sibling rivalry,' offered Vince, staring deep into Armitage's curiously asymmetric eyes. 'The lorry is a symbol of the mother love that Zachary feels should have been his, but was diverted on to you. He's trying to take back what he feels you stole from him, by projecting complex, half-understood emotions onto an object he knows is of personal value to you.' Vince had done a GCSE in psychology during his time in Grimwood Scrubs.

'**WHAT ARE YOU TALKING ABOUT?**' snapped Zachary and Armitage together. '**MOTHER LOVE? WE NEVER GOT ANY MOTHER LOVE! ALL SHE CARED ABOUT WAS HER PET NEWTS.**'

'This is very positive,' said Vince. 'Tell me more about your mother.'

After this one final job, he was planning to train as a therapist.

'**POSITIVE? SHE HATED US! NO CUDDLES! NO PRESENTS!**' yelled the two brothers, before turning to face each other, growling and recommencing their bicker.

'No presents?' yelled Zachary. 'What are you talking about? She bought you seven hundred and thirty-two tiny enormous lorries and never bought me a single one!'

'Only because you kept breaking them all!'

'It was the only way I could get any attention! If I wasn't smashing your tiny enormous lorries she would just disappear to be with her newts.'

'I hated those newts!'

'Me, too.'

'So perhaps some of the anger you channelled towards each other, driving you apart, was in fact a shared anger towards your mother's newts,' said

Vince. 'I think this is an important breakthrough.'

'I HATED THOSE NEWTS!' yelled Zachary and Armitage, in unison, again.

'Excellent,' said Vince. 'This is great. Let it all out.'

At that moment, Hannah and Billy arrived on the scene. They were stunned by what they saw. Two Armitages! One of them was dressed in burglarising gear, but with the coating of squid ink now replaced by a shiny layer of camel goo. The other one was dressed as ringmaster from the waist up, but on his lower half was wearing nothing except a pair of boxer shorts decorated with pictures of toy lorries.

This would have been strange enough but, to make it even weirder, they were both weeping, and shouting at the top of their voices, 'I HATED THOSE NEWTS! I HATED THOSE NEWTS! I HATED THOSE NEWTS!'

This was not what Hannah and Billy had been expecting to find.

'Which one's Armitage?' whispered Hannah.

'It must be the gooey one. We saw him earlier.'

'Unless the one we saw earlier wasn't the real Armitage, but we just assumed it was because we didn't know there were two of them.'

'You could be right.'

'I can't believe there's two of them,' said Hannah. 'Of all the people for there to be two of, why did it have to be Armitage Shank?'

Nee naw, nee naw! A siren cut through the air and they all turned to see a police car swerving across the marshes.

Hannah rushed forward and waved it to a stop. She jabbered at the policeman as he stepped out, 'He's right here! Armitage Shank! He's been on the run for years. Except now there's two of him!'

'Is this a prank call?' said the policeman, on the brink of getting back into his car.

'No! Come quickly! Please!'

The policeman did come, but he didn't hurry.

He was not impressed with this whole scenario, which seemed beneath his dignity.

When he saw the two Shanks weeping and shouting about newts, his level of impressed-ness sank even further.

'Young lady, was it you who reported a crime?' he asked Hannah.

'Yes! Him! Over there! One of him is Armitage Shank, legendary burglariser and escaped criminal! Scourge of the nation! Disgrace to the circus fraternity!'

'Which one?'

'I'm not sure.'

Armitage and Zachary had just experienced a major breakthrough. They'd stopped shouting about newts, had carried on weeping, but were now engaged in a deep hug. The last time they'd hugged was in the womb. Which was a while ago. And even then, it was more due to a lack of space than through any genuine fondness.

'This is very significant,' said Vince. 'Would you like to draw a picture of your feelings?'

'Oi!' said the policeman. 'Which one of you is Armitage Shank?'

The two of them broke out of the hug, and at the sight of a police uniform the old instincts quickly kicked back in.

'Him!' they both said, pointing at one another.

It had been a moving, but brief, reconciliation.

'Which of you owns that lorry?' asked the policeman, pointing up at the 'Shank's Impossible Circus' lorry.

'Him!' said Armitage and Zachary, pointing at one another.

'Which of you owns that van?' asked the policeman, pointing at the **'ZACHARY SHANK ENTERPRISES: DUCKING/DIVING, IMPORT/ EXPORT, BARGAIN DESIGNERWEAR, DVDS,**

PERFUME. BESPOKE LOAN SERVICES ALSO AVAILABLE' van.

'Me!' said Armitage and Zachary.

At this moment, the policeman noticed Ewan.

'Who are you?' demanded the policeman.

'Er . . . I'm a policeman,' said Ewan.

'I've never seen you before. What's your name?'

'Inspector Hector Spector. From Scotland Yard. And I've never seen you before. What's your name?'

'Constable Runcible Constable. Also from Scotland Yard. And I have a good mind to arrest you for impersonating a police officer.'

'Well, I've a good mind to arrest you for impersonating a police officer,' countered Ewan, who knew from his boxing days that attack was often the best form of defence.

'If you're from Scotland Yard,' said Constable Runcible Constable, 'how come you're wearing an

American police uniform?'

'Is this American?' said Ewan. 'Oh, blast. I knew

something was wrong.'

'THEY'RE ESCAPING!' yelled Hannah, drawing Constable Runcible Constable's attention to the fact that the two Armitages were now running away across the marshes.

'YOU TWO!' yelled the constable. 'Stop right there!'

They didn't stop.

Constable Runcible Constable took out his police whistle and blew, his cheeks puffing like an amorous frog.

Both Armitages continued to run away.

'This is not an ordinary whistle,' shouted Constable Runcible Constable, 'it is a police whistle! And it is commanding you to come back here!'

Neither Armitage stopped running.

Constable Runcible Constable blew again, even louder, which made him look like an amorous purple frog wearing too much make-up. *PEEEEEEEEEP!* 'This whistle carries the full authority of Her Majesty's Metropolitan Police Authority! Which is a lot of authority.' *PEEEEEP! PEEEEEP!* 'And it is commanding you to stop running!'

The Armitages ignored him.

'This is not a request! It is an order!' *PEEEEEE EEEEEEEEEEEEEEEEEEEEEEEEEP!*

You can probably guess the effect of this order. Zilch. The Armitages were now approaching the edge of Hockney Marshes, on the verge of disappearing out of sight.

'You're only making things worse for yourself! Ignoring a police whistle is a criminal offence!'

But on they ran.

'I don't think your whistle is having the desired effect,' said Hannah. 'They're getting away.'

'That's the trouble with criminals,' sighed

Constable Runcible Constable. 'They have no respect for the law. It makes my job extremely difficult.'

'The whistle you need is one of these,' said Billy. He put the first two fingers of each hand into his mouth and blew. An extraordinary sound came out: a soaring, scooping, screeching squeal that sounded like a cross between a pneumatic drill, an air raid siren and six thousand flautists practising their scales.

The windows on Constable Runcible Constable's car shattered. Ten squirrels fell unconscious out of nearby trees. Ewan Hoozarmy did a very small wee in his pants. And a passing dog, which in normal circumstances would have immediately started running after the unconscious squirrels, froze to the spot and spontaneously gave birth, which was particularly surprising since it was male.

But more important than these strangely

unscientific side-effects was the response from a certain camel, who until that point had been dozing contentedly between the Big Tops. Narcissus didn't just wake up; he did something very unusual. He did something that camels only do in a crisis, when specially trained to respond to an emergency signal. Narcissus sprang upright and galloped. He galloped directly towards Billy without even pausing for a second to contemplate the location of the nearest supply of taramasalata.

'How do you do that?' said Constable Runcible Constable.

'I'll teach you later,' said Billy. 'We have to catch Armitage Shank! Both of him! They're getting away!'

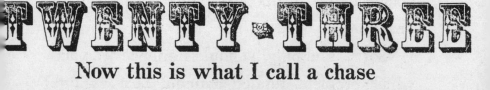

TWENTY-THREE

Now this is what I call a chase

NARCISSUS DREW UP IN FRONT OF BILLY and went down on his knees. Billy mounted him swiftly.

'Hop on,' he said to Hannah. 'I'm going to need some help.'

Hannah hopped on.

Narcissus stood up.

Hannah fell off.

Billy had forgotten to tell Hannah that when

camels stand up they straighten their back legs first, the result of which was that Hannah somersaulted all the way down his neck to the ground.

'Sorry,' said Billy. 'I should have warned you.'

'No problem,' replied Hannah. 'That was fun.'

Narcissus was still angled downwards, so Hannah ran back up his neck, sat on the front hump, and this time held on tight while he straightened his front legs and set off at a renewed gallop, in pursuit of the Shank twins. You may recall that riding Narcissus felt like sitting on a seesaw strapped to a supermarket trolley rolling around the deck of a boat on a stormy day in the middle of the Atlantic. And that's when he was walking. Riding a galloping camel was like being picked up by a giant who has mistaken you for a piggy bank and is trying to shake out a stuck penny. This was not what car salesmen describe as a 'smooth ride'.

'You steer,' said Billy, who was now standing on the rear hump.

'How do I do that?' replied Hannah, gripping Narcissus' neck with all her might.

'Oh, he knows where he's going. But if he sees any food he might veer off course and you'll have to yank the reins.'

'There aren't any reins.'

'Aren't there? Oh, well. We'll just have to hope for the best. Do you mind if I use your head for balance?'

'Go ahead.'

Billy, still standing, undid the rope that was holding up his trousers and fashioned it into a lasso. Once the lasso was made, he whirled it around his head and yelled, 'Yeeee haaaah!' like a cowboy – or, rather, a camelboy. A camelboy whose trousers had, unsurprisingly, fallen down to reveal the bottom half of his Lycra star-spangled circus costume.

Local passers-by, out for an evening stroll, were

rather surprised by this sight. But we're not interested in them right now.

Narcissus, Hannah and Billy soon caught up with the Shanks, just as they reached the edge of the marshes and began sprinting down Hockney High Street.

'That idiotic boy and his idiotic friend on their idiotic camel are coming after us,' spat Armitage. 'We'd better split up. You go left, I'll go right.'

'You're always bossing me around. Why don't you go left and I'll go right?' replied Zachary.

'MAKE WAY! MAKE WAY! COMING THROUGH!' yelled Hannah to passing shoppers, who were having to fling themselves off the pavement to avoid the galloping camel. 'SORRY! POLICE EMERGENCY.'

'What do you mean, "bossing you around"?' said Armitage. 'I'm just saying we should split up so they can't catch us both.'

'You've been bossing me around all my life!'

'Well, at least I'm not a thief,' said Armitage.

'Yes, you are. It's your job.'

'Not from you. You're the one that kept on stealing my tiny enormous lorry!'

'You started it!'

'You started it.'

And while the Shank twins returned to their favourite bicker, a lasso whirled through the air, circling above their heads.

But just as it was about to ensnare them, something extraordinary happened. A swarm of canaries arrived and caught the lasso in their beaks.

How on earth, you may wonder, could this possibly have happened? Well, it's quite simple. A little unusual, granted, but perfectly explicable. You see, Narcissus wasn't the only mammal to hear Billy's emergency whistle. Maurice had been just beginning an evening massage on the roof of his caravan when this call, immediately followed by the unmistakable sound of galloping camel hooves, alerted him to the danger that was facing his employer.

Knowing that (despite being one of the fittest specimens of masculinity in the civilised world) he could never catch a galloping camel, Maurice had dashed to his canary choir, whose training in the art of criminal techniques had been coming on very nicely. He unlatched the door of their cage and commanded them to 'STOP THAT CAMEL!'

Irrrrena had jumped down from their roof at the same time, with a similar idea. She hurried to 3.14159's pen, unlocked the door, and instructed him to give chase. The pig looked up at her with an expression which communicated that he was both unimpressed and peckish. 3.14159 ambled off in the direction of the Big Top, pausing on the way to eat a guy rope.

Fingers, having roughly the same idea, had released his monkeys.

'Follow that camel!' he shouted.

Monday ran north; Tuesday ran south; Wednesday ran east; Thursday ran west; Friday put one thumb in each ear and jumped up and down on the spot, shouting, 'ACK ACK ACK OOK OOK ACK.' Cuddlecakes jumped into Fingers' arms and gave him a cuddle. The training of the monkeys was not at an advanced stage.

The canaries, however, followed Maurice's instructions perfectly and even improvised a strategy of their own, which is why, only a few minutes later, Billy found himself in a strange tug of war. The flock of canaries were now trying to pull him off Narcissus' back. Billy had never wrestled a canary choir before, but they were a surprisingly strong team. He could feel his foothold on Narcissus' rear hump weakening.

'Hold my legs, Hannah!' he said. 'And sing the "Marseillaise".'

'The "Marseillaise"?' replied Hannah. A patriotic sing-song was not what she had in mind for this particular moment.

'Yes, it's the French national anthem.'

'I know, but . . .'

Billy began to sing:

France is really cool,
Oooh, yeah.
Much, much cooler than everywhere else.
With really nice cheese and everything,
Oooh, so cool, so so cool.

Hannah didn't know the words, but she la-la-laed along to the tune. She didn't know the tune, either, to be honest, but she tried her best. Just as Billy hoped, the canaries immediately joined in, their beaks gaping wide to lustily intone every word. This caused them to drop the rope.

Back on firm ground – or firm hump – Billy swung the lasso above his head again, still singing, and hurled it one more time in the direction of the Shank twins, who were still running and still bickering – now, seemingly, about newts. The lasso looped perfectly over the twins' heads, descended past the two moustaches and two sets of hideous teeth, and gripped the brothers around the waist.

'Whooaaaah there,' yelled Billy.

Narcissus skidded to a halt. The Shanks crashed to the ground. Hannah flew through the air, and only saved herself from entering a passing double-decker bus through a top-floor window by grabbing hold of a lamp-post, halfway up.

'Yeeeee-haaaah!' said Billy, dismounting from Narcissus, who was now entirely blocking the entrance to the Hockney High Street branch of

Poundstretcher.

The canaries watched through their disappointed little canary eyes, but continued gamely on into the second verse of the French national anthem, which was about wine and long-distance cycling.

Narcissus smiled, something he hadn't done for seventeen years.

'How could you plot against me like this?' wailed Armitage, attempting unsuccessfully to get back on his feet. 'After everything I did for you?'

'What, killing my mother, imprisoning my father and forcing me to participate in your criminal schemes?' replied Billy.

'No, the other stuff. Giving you a job and leftover food and occasionally nicking clothes for you from charity shops.'

'You never even paid me.'

'That would have been illegal. You were

underage.'

'The job was as a thief! And I never wanted to steal. I never wanted to be part of your hideous, disgraceful excuse for a circus. You're a traitor to the circus fraternity, Armitage, a common criminal, and now you're going where you belong. Prison.'

'Did you say common? How dare you call me common?' barked Armitage.

Billy had never before spoken his mind to Armitage, not even once, and it left him feeling rather light-headed. His brain now felt empty of all words.

'He said you're a common criminal. Which you are,' said Hannah, who was sliding back to earth, down the lamp-post.

'It's all your fault,' snapped Armitage, pointing a long, bony and still slightly fishy finger in her direction. 'You've corrupted him. You've made him . . . honest.'

'He was honest already. In his heart. He just needed some help. Billy's the bravest—'

'Oh, vomit vomit vomit, I don't want to hear any of that you're-so-wonderful nonsense. Being tied up with this moron is bad enough without having to listen to you two bang on about how wonderful you think you are. Didn't anyone ever teach you it's bad manners to gloat?'

'No,' said Billy. 'You taught me to gloat as loudly as possible at every opportunity.'

'That's different!' snapped Armitage.

This is when Wednesday appeared (the Shanks had been running east). Recognising Armitage, Wednesday ran towards him and gleefully jumped up and down on his head, shouting, 'ACK ACK ACK OOK OOK ACK', which means . . . well, nothing really, except perhaps, 'Hello, I feel like jumping up and down on your head.'

'Did you just call me a moron?' said Zachary,

who seemed in something of a daze, as if he couldn't quite understand what had just happened to him.

'*Did you just call me a moron?*' replied Armitage, wrestling Wednesday into an arm lock.

'Are you making fun of my voice?'

'*Are you making fun of my voice?*' said Armitage, who now seemed to be in an arm lock himself, with Wednesday wrapped around his back.

'That's not funny.'

'Just get this monkey off me!'

'Why should I?'

While the Shank twins argued, moaned and wrestled with Wednesday, Billy tied the lasso to Narcissus' tail and led the way back towards Hockney Marshes.

The canaries were now on the seventh verse of the French national anthem, which was about high-speed trains and an unfortunate head-butting incident during a World Cup final.

TWENTY-FOUR

The arrest. Justice at last! Or maybe not . . .

CONSTABLE RUNCIBLE CONSTABLE WAS still standing by his car, gazing forlornly at the broken windows. He was attempting to fill in an accident report form. So far he'd written:

I was proceeding in a northerly direction on the evening of the 1ˢᵗ January, responding to an emergency call from a distressed citizen of a possibly juvenile persuasion involving circus-related thievery, when a boy from said entertainment troupe whistled to summon his trained camel in order to chase and lasso two escaping twin ringmasters who were suspects in the above case. As a result of the volume and high frequency of the aforementioned whistle . . .

There was something wrong with this report that Constable Runcible Constable couldn't put his finger on. The punctuation wasn't right. And he wasn't sure why, but he had a feeling his boss might not believe him.

For a moment he couldn't believe it himself. Then the boy and the camel and the girl and the two ringmaster twins, now roped together and accompanied by a surprisingly cheerful monkey, appeared in front of him.

'We've done your job for you,' said Billy. 'You can arrest them now.'

'Er . . . what for?' replied Constable Runcible Constable, who didn't have a very good memory. In fact, he didn't have a very good anything. He was, as the saying goes, an idiot.

'I called 999 to report a robbery,' said Hannah. 'It was him that did it! Armitage Shank!'

'That's right!' said Constable Runcible Constable. 'Robbery! Safe blown up in the box office of a Big Top. You're one of the suspects. You're two of the suspects. You two are both one of the suspects. Something like that.'

'But we have an alibi,' said Armitage. 'I've been with him all day.'

'Yes, me too,' said Zachary. 'We've been catching up on old times. We're brothers.'

'Apart from when I was on stage,' added Armitage, realising that he couldn't claim to have been in two places at once.

'You were on stage?' said Hannah. 'Then you must be Armitage!'

'No – by the stage. It felt like I was on stage, because I was so close, in the front row, and so nervous for my brother, but I was by the stage, watching him perform. He was wonderful.'

'Thank you,' said Zachary. 'I mean – no! Lies! I was by the stage! He was on the stage.'

At this point, Ernesto appeared.

As soon as his show finished, Ernesto had run off in search of Hannah and Billy to check they were safe. Knowing Armitage was on the loose, he hadn't wanted to risk leaving the night's box-office takings lying around, so he'd shoved all the money into a backpack and taken it with him.

Now, to his huge relief, he'd found them. So pleased was he to find them unharmed that he barely noticed the two policemen and two

Armitages who were also right there.

The instant Armitage saw Ernesto, carrying a backpack, his nose twitched with a spontaneous, cunning upsurge of thief's instinct. He could recognise a sack of loot from fifty paces, blindfold, with seven balaclavas over his head, and he sensed in his inner criminal nervous system that there was something fishy about Ernesto's backpack. Something roughly as fishy as a safe filled with squid ink.

This had been a day of bad plans badly executed. But now one last plan occurred to him, masterful in its simplicity.

'There he is!' said Armitage. 'That's the man! Stop him! He blew up my safe!'

'Him?' said Constable Runcible Constable.

'Yes! All my night's takings! He got away with the whole lot!'

'What are you talking about?' said Ernesto. 'He

blew up my safe. But I knew he was going to, so I filled it with rancid squid ink. He's the thief.'

'And you're accusing him of stealing rancid squid ink?' said the constable.

'He's the thief!' said Armitage, raising an accusing finger towards Ernesto. 'Look in his bag!'

Ernesto's legs suddenly turned to lead, as he realised what Armitage had done. He was carrying hundreds of pounds in used banknotes. Armitage had framed him. Again.

Constable Runcible Constable stepped forward and looked inside Ernesto's backpack. It was, indeed, stuffed with cash.

'Right! You're under arrest!'

At that moment, Wanda appeared. She'd been looking for Hannah ever since the end of the circus, but she hadn't been doing it very well, since her head was filled with dreamy soft-focus images of Ernesto back-flipping through flaming hoops. It was only when she finally caught sight of Hannah that her head cleared and she remembered who she was and what she was supposed to be doing.

'WHAT'S GOING ON?' she demanded. 'HANNAH! I've been looking for you everywhere! My parking has almost expired, and if we don't

head home very soon you might miss your bedtime, which as we both know puts you in a very bad mood the next day.'

As usual, Wanda and Hannah were not on the same wavelength. 'There are two Armitages!' said Hannah. 'We lassoed them to stop them escaping, but now one of them has framed Ernesto! That policeman's trying to arrest him for stealing his own money, because Armitage has told him it's his money when it isn't!'

'Do you have a fever, dear?' said Wanda, feeling Hannah's forehead. 'I knew it was a bad idea for you to go up on that stage. You sound delirious. I think today has been far too much for you. Well, at least you've got that circus nonsense out of your system now, and we can go back home and find you a more sensible hobby.'

'Look for yourself! Two Armitages!'

Wanda looked. Hannah was right. Apart from

Narcissus' tongue, she had never seen anything quite so unpleasant.

Hannah leaped forward towards Constable Runcible Constable, who was now putting handcuffs on Ernesto.

'This is totally unfair!' she yelled. 'Why are you arresting him? That's his own money! You can't steal your own money!'

'A theft has been reported and he's the suspect, because he's carrying stolen currency.'

'IT'S HIS MONEY!'

'If it's his money he's carrying around, nobody would have reported a theft. And people don't just carry around huge bags of cash.'

'I'm carrying it to stop him robbing me!' pleaded Ernesto, pointing at Armitage. 'Or maybe him,' he added, pointing at Zachary.

'He's trying to frame me! The outrage!' said Armitage. 'Blackmail! You can add that to the charge sheet.'

'**THIS IS ARMITAGE SHANK!**' yelled Hannah. '**HE'S WANTED BY EVERY POLICE FORCE IN THE COUNTRY. OR MAYBE THAT'S HIM! BUT ONE OF THEM IS! YOU CAN'T LET THEM GO FREE!**'

'I've found who I was after, young lady,' said Constable Runcible Constable, 'and I'll thank you not to tell me how to do my job. Whether he's innocent or not is a matter for the courts. And the rest of you had better watch it. I don't want any more nonsense.'

'Of course not, officer,' said Armitage. 'Shall I help you with your car door? There you go, officer. Thank you so much. You're doing a wonderful job.'

Constable Runcible Constable gave Armitage a suspicious stare. 'What did you say your name was?'

'Nothing! Nobody! Er . . . Gabriel Honeytoes. I

just help out in a menial capacity at the circus. Sweeping up. Folding costumes. Struggling to rub two pennies together in the humble service of art. Anyway, I'm rambling. Must be off. Bye.'

And with that he climbed up into his enormous lorry and without so much as a 'see you in another twenty years' to his long-lost brother, roared away. Or tried to.

After a long, whinnying splutter from the enormous engine of the enormous lorry, Armitage reappeared, carrying a jerry can.

'Anyone know where the nearest petrol station is?' he asked. Constable Runcible Constable was still giving him that hostile stare. 'Never mind. I'll find one.'

And away he ran.

After a few paces, he stopped and turned back.

'If a traffic warden comes, tell him it's a medical emergency and I'll be right back.'

And away he ran, again.

After a few more paces, he stopped and turned back once more. Constable Runcible Constable was still giving him that stare.

'I mean, tell him nothing but the truth – which is my policy in all matters of law enforcement. And you can say that I'll pay the fine with exceptional promptness,' said Armitage.

And away he ran, yet again. This time he didn't stop.

At the same time, Zachary, Frankie, Vince, Chippy and Ewan climbed into their van and sped off, unaware that Wednesday was on the roof, nibbling a recently detached windscreen wiper.

Constable Runcible Constable bundled Ernesto into the police car.

'You've got the wrong man!' pleaded Hannah. 'The real criminals are getting away. They were right here and you're letting them escape!'

Billy just stared. He couldn't speak. He couldn't watch his father being taken away from him again.

'Young lady,' said Constable Runcible Constable, leaning through the broken window, 'I'm a professional law enforcement officer, and believe you me, I know a criminal when I— OW! OW! OW! That's really sharp!' He paused to pick a fragment of glass out of his elbow, then carried on his speech, this time with his arm inside the car. 'As I was saying, professional law enforcement, blah blah blah, know a criminal when I see one, and this chap in the back of my car, he's a wrong 'un through and through. I can tell from the eyes. And from the bag of stolen money he's carrying.'

'It's not stolen!'

'Not to mention those witnesses.'

'They're liars!'

'We'll see about that. Mark my words.'

'Which words?'

'All of them.' Constable Runcible Constable revved the engine, put on the siren, and took off at speed. Backwards. He wasn't very good at gears.

There was a loud crunch as he hunted for first gear. Or second gear. Just any of the forward ones would be fine.

'I'll be OK!' called Ernesto, out of the back window. 'Don't worry about me! Take care of yourself, Billy. Stay safe and stay honest. I'll come back for you as soon as I can! Look after him, Hannah! And never forget that you're circus!'

With those words, Ernesto was driven away to an uncertain fate, leaving us very little time indeed to salvage anything remotely resembling a happy ending from this messy farrago of injustice, indignity, ineptitude, badly trained monkeys and canary-obstructed-twin-ringmaster-lassoing.

TWENTY-FIVE

Poor Billy. Silly Billy. Lucky Billy?

POOR BILLY.

Yet again, his father had been dragged away from him, framed for a crime he hadn't committed.

Billy slumped to the ground. Hannah sat next to him and put an arm around his shoulders.

Hannah's touch lifted Billy's spirits a little, yet it was also the trigger for the beginnings of a snuffle. He didn't exactly cry, but he wasn't quite not crying, either. Billy was feeling very sorry for himself, and with good reason.

Wanda was feeling sorry for him, too, which wasn't a sensation she liked. She wasn't fond of being in any situation where she had to converse with a human who washed less than six times a week. Billy, by the look of him, washed less than six times a month.

'Do you have anywhere to go?' asked Wanda.

Billy shook his head.

'Armitage will be back when he finds some petrol. You could join up with him again, couldn't you? Until your father gets out. I'm sure Ernesto will clear his name.'

Billy shrugged.

'Why don't you come and live with us?' said Hannah.

Billy looked up, but didn't reply.

Wanda's face puckered into a lemon-sucking pout. 'Hannah! What a ridiculous idea! Ha ha ha! She's joking! What a silly joke! Don't pay any attention to her, Billy. She has the weirdest sense of humour. You! In our house! Hahahahaha!'

'Billy can share my room. He can *have* my room,' pleaded Hannah. 'We can't just leave him here.'

'He has a father of his own. He has two fathers. He has an ample supply of fathers. We can't go around taking children off the street and dragging them off to live with us! That's just . . . not possible.'

'He's not a random child off the street. He's my brother. My at-least-half-brother.'

'But what about the other half of him? He's not like us! He's a circus child! He's half-wild. He probably has nits.'

'*I'm* a circus child,' said Hannah.

'You think you're a circus child but you're actually very well brought up, with immaculately clean hair.'

'He needs help.'

'I'm fine,' said Billy. 'I can go back and work for Armitage. I could never go where I'm not wanted.'

'You *are* wanted! We want you to come!' insisted Hannah.

'Don't worry. I wouldn't belong.'

Hannah turned from Billy to Wanda, grabbed her arms, and stared deep into her eyes with a hypnotic gaze that sent a spooky that-really-reminds-me-of-my-sister shiver down Wanda's spine, back up her spine, twice around her skull, then out of her left ear. 'Pleeeeeaaaaaaaaase!' Hannah begged. 'We have to!'

'There simply isn't space,' said Wanda. 'I'm sorry.'

As soon as these words were out of Wanda's mouth, her phone beeped with a text message from Granny, which said: Of course there's space.

Wanda sighed and typed frantically into her phone. 'This is none of your business. And he's half-wild. He'd cause chaos.'

Granny responded immediately, in capitals: HE'S FAMILY. HANNAH'S RIGHT. YOU HAVE TO TAKE HIM IN.

Wanda switched off her phone and shoved it deep into her handbag. She looked at Billy and sighed.

'I'm not keen on this at all,' said Wanda, after a

long think. 'You'd have to wash. Regularly. Including your hair.'

Hannah leaped up and gave her a limb-crushing hug.

'We'll need to incinerate those clothes,' added Wanda, who found to her surprise that she seemed to be smiling. Wanda very rarely did anything she didn't want to do, and was interested to notice the oddly pleasurable sensation that went with making a reckless decision you weren't quite sure was the right one.

'Billy?' said Hannah. 'Will you come home with us?'

'To your house?' said Billy. He said the word 'house' as if he barely knew how to pronounce it.

'Yes,' replied Hannah, reaching out a hand and pulling him up.

'I've never slept in a house before,' he said. 'Is it really hot? I don't like being hot.'

'It's cosy,' said Wanda. 'It's just right.'

'We can turn down the heating if you feel uncomfortable,' offered Hannah.

'I don't think I can. I'm circus. A . . . house?'

'What, you'd rather be stuck with Armitage again, stealing for a living?'

'No! That's the last thing I want! Joint last. Level with being stuck in one place every day in a building without any wheels.'

'That's crazy! Didn't you listen to what Ernesto said? Stay safe and stay honest. The only way you can do that is with us.'

'Mmmmm. I don't know. Could I bring Narcissus?'

'No,' said Wanda. 'Absolutely not. No no no no no no no no no no no no no. NO!'

'I think that was a no,' said Hannah.

'You'll have to ask one of your circus people to take care of him,' said Wanda. 'There must be someone.'

'I think you'd like him. He's very friendly,' said Billy, attempting a charming smile, which didn't really have the desired effect, because all Wanda noticed was the tooth decay.

'We hardly use the garden shed. He could go in there,' suggested Hannah. 'He really is very friendly.'

'No. No no no no no no no no no no no no no. NO!'

As a rule, it wasn't easy to change Wanda's mind. A spreadsheet enumerating counterbalanced lists of pros and cons was usually the only way to get her to reassess her position on anything. It will therefore come as a surprise to you that Wanda was soon on the phone to her husband demanding that he clear out the garden shed to make way for a camel, and clear out the spare room to make way for a boy.

I can't really explain how Hannah and Billy did it. Billy thought it might have something to do with Narcissus appearing at the crucial moment and giving Wanda an irresistibly charismatic glance with those movie-star eyes, but then Billy was biased. Hannah thought that maybe seeing her perform had made Wanda realise the family really were circus.

In truth, even Wanda didn't quite know why she agreed to it, except to say that for the first time ever, she found herself wondering whether life might be more interesting if you weren't quite in control of what happened all the time. A hint of chaos might not, after all, be a catastrophe. Wanda was perhaps, as Hannah had guessed, detecting the faintest glimmer of her inner circus. Either that, or she'd gone nuts.

Billy still didn't feel right about living in a

house, and before they'd even set off, he was already wondering when would be the best time to ask about moving into the shed with Narcissus.

How long could he really last as a civilian? He'd lived a life of non-stop fly-by-night circussing, with frequent midnight flits, dawn raids and daylight robberies. He'd never stayed in one place for longer than a week. But after everything he'd lived through, the prospect facing him now felt like the strangest adventure of all.

'My father will come back, won't he?' asked Billy, even though Hannah and Wanda knew no more than he did.

'Of course,' said Hannah.

'Hopefully very soon,' added Wanda.

'We're just looking after you for a short while until he sets the record straight,' said Hannah. 'Think of it as a holiday.'

'Think of it as market research. It's your chance

to find out how normal people think,' added Wanda.

'Just come,' said Hannah. 'I'm your sister. You're my brother. It's the most natural thing in the world.'

'Then why does it feel so weird?'

Hannah and Wanda shrugged, smiled and reached out to him. Billy thought for a second, then reached out in return, holding on to his sister with one hand and his aunt with the other.

Together, in step, they set off away from Hockney Marshes, towards Billy's new life, arriving very soon at the place known, for now, as . . .

...THE END

Except that . . .

A few questions . . .

Remain.

1 – How long can Billy survive in a house?

2 – How long can Wanda survive with a Billy?

3 – Will Hannah ever go fully circus?

4 – Will Ernesto be convicted of stealing his own money?

5 – What dastardly scheme will Armitage cook up next?

6 – What will Narcissus eat next?

7 – What is the mystery of the spoons?

8 – What would happen if Tuesdays didn't exist?

9 – What is the highest mountain in Belgium

CAN'T GET ENOUGH OF ARMITAGE SHANK AND HIS ROTTEN CIRCUS? THEN MAKE SURE YOU LOOK OUT FOR...